OUR ABIDING HERITAGE

OUR ABIDING HERITAGE

A COLLECTION OF DIVERSE SHORT STORIES

C.D. SUTHERLAND   PRISCILLA ADAMS

JANN FRANKLIN   MARGUERITE MARTIN GRAY

CAROLE LEHR JOHNSON   BEVERLY FLANDERS

TINA MIDDLETON   CALVIN HUBBARD

MARY LOU CHEATHAM   SUSAN HIERS FOSTER

Our Abiding Heritage:

A Collection of Diverse Short Stories

Published by Narrow Way Press LLC
www.narrowwaypress.com

Paperback ISBN: 978-1-937366-36-0

Hardback ISBN: 978-1-937366-37-7

eBook ISBN: 978-1-937366-38-4

4 5 6 7 8 9 10

DEDICATION

This book is dedicated to Jesus Christ, who is God incarnate; salvation comes through Him alone. He created everything that was ever created. Because He loves us so much, He became a human being, died by crucifixion in payment for our sins, was buried, rose on the third day, ascended to Heaven, lives today, and will come again to this earth; believers in Him shall be bodily resurrected to begin a new, undying life, and He will reign as King of kings and Lord of lords over His new creation forever.

ABOUT OUR ABIDING HERITAGE

C.D. SUTHERLAND

Our Heritage

Nailed to a cross so rough,
Amazing, it was enough.

My family's heritage can bless or do worse,
Especially when it's a family curse.

Be a loser or a beauty queen,
Maybe there's something in between.

We may cross over the blue sea,
To discover whence came Lucy.

Blood is thicker than water,
But family is more than what's inside us.

Our heritage may be proven a fable,
Through a picture and note in a table.

If we could slip through time,
Christ would still pay our fine.

Books are passed like a baton;
Now it's my race to carry on.

Still searching for the answer;
What happened with the panther?

My muse can come from a spark,
But also from a fear of the dark.

This publication is a testimony of the sixth year a group of authors assembled their collective muse to create an anthology celebrating the short story. The last five years' collections, *Celebrating the Short Story, Over the Moon Travel Treasures, 2020 Vision, Coming of Age,* and *Second Chances,* contributed significantly to advancing the craft of Christian fiction writing. This year, ten authors have collaborated to produce the outstanding collection of diverse short stories you're now viewing, *Our Abiding Heritage.*

The short story has long endured since the creation of language. It is a good vehicle for presenting an account, more often concentrating on creating a mood rather than a plot. A short story can range from a cleverly crafted sentence up to 20,000 words. Whatever the length, a short story is typically centered around one plot, one main character, and one central theme. This contrasts with a novel's capacity to weave multiple plots and themes among an array of notable characters. The writing styles used in short stories can be somewhat unusual or surprising to their readers. Sometimes their writers use literary techniques which might wear down a reader if employed throughout the length of a novel. Being short, by definition, they provide the perfect fodder for being assembled into collections, usually with some unifying theme or common element to tie them together.

The ten short stories in *Our Abiding Heritage* are as diverse in technique and theme as our previous years' writings; nevertheless, they are united in the fact that a heritage element is common. We invite you to take notice of the techniques used by this array of talented authors to weave those heritage-related appearances into their stories.

These ten adventures will take you to places you have never been. C.D. Sutherland's *Enough* takes you to Golgotha and the crucifixion of Christ as witnessed through the eyes of Stephanus Longinus, a young Roman soldier. Priscilla Adams' debut short story *Generational Curse* drops you into the chaos of a fast-paced love affair, where the soon-to-be bride discovers her fiancé's family curse. Jann Franklin's *The Backup Beauty Queen* pulls you into small-town Louisiana festival culture, where family, enthusiasm, and talent collide with laughter. Marguerite Martin Gray's *The Thread Uncovered* examines a tendril through Sophie Lucy Marteen's life, revealing how family relationships do not always require blood ties. Carole Lehr Johnson's *Heritage of Hope* takes you to seventeenth-century England to show how Melior Olford, a character in her 2022 release, *The Burning Sands,* came to be married to Radigan Atwood. Beverly Flanders' *Katherine's Table* plunges you into a mystery as a family heirloom reveals its secrets to Katie and her cousin Laura. Tina Ann Middleton's *Lord of Time* places you on a time-traveling adventure where a good-intentioned man named Chad strives to rescue Jesus from the cross. Should he succeed, what would be the ramifications of that? Calvin Hubbard's debut fiction, *The Handoff,* takes you on Tom's nostalgic journey where he realizes specific events from key players in his life gave him precisely what he needed to run the race set before him. Mary Lou Cheatham's *Crossing Cohay Branch* ventures into the recesses of a childhood memory, generating as many questions as it answers. Finally, Susan Hiers Foster's *Out of the Dark* follows an author's quest for inspiration in Maine, where she meets a famous author who needs something from her.

When you return from these experiences, chances are some will have left you wanting more. If so, check out that story's author page at the back of the book. They might have something else you'll like. We believe you'll be glad you did.

ENOUGH

C.D. SUTHERLAND

The walk from the Antonia Fortress to the Place of the Skulls was neither long nor steep unless one were compelled to bear a heavy, rough-hewn crossbeam. Even more so if the walker had suffered a flogging, especially if it were the type of punishment we Romans reserved for murderers and traitors. Such a scourging involved the flagellum, a short, wicked whip of multiple leather straps knotted with shards of metal and bone, all connected to a sturdy handle. The brutal tool was notorious for tearing off flesh and exposing veins, bowels, and often the bone beneath. Its purpose was to be horrible so that on-lookers would be encouraged to behave and thus not commit similar crimes against the Roman Empire.

That made this man's plight absurd because he had committed no crimes.

My name is Stephanus Longinus, a young and respected legionary in the Antonia cohort, which serves Emperor Tiberius. My keen ears heard the Prefect of Judaea, Pontius Pilate, shout to the chattering mob of black-robed priests, "I find no fault in him!"

What could be more understandable than that? He was already

bleeding and battered so thoroughly that most men would be writhing in pain, crumpled on the floor, begging for mercy or even death. Still, somehow this man, a rabbi, a mere teacher, managed to stand straight and face them with his mask of blood and ragged folds of flesh. The scourging wasn't enough for his tormentors.

An additional injury had been thrust upon him by a mock crown made of those needle-sharp native thorns of Judaea, noted for wounding our horses. When tasked to flog this man, whom the local priests despised, my fellow legionaries wanted him to suffer greatly for pretending to be a king. You'd think that would have been enough to satisfy those priests and the mob that followed them, but it didn't. This man's life had driven them stark-raving mad.

"Crucify him!"

Their words echoed off the masonry walls surrounding the pavement. The Jewish crowd insisted no other punishment would suffice, even though it was a uniquely Roman technique used on non-citizens, primarily slaves and rebels. I'd been told that before Roman rule prevented them from killing each other, the Jews preferred to stone their offenders. They'd surround their target and hurl rocks in a mob-like frenzy until the victim died, or at least until the effort extinguished their emotional fervor.

Barbarians.

Initially, the priests had accused the man of having claimed to be a god, which they called blasphemy. While it was no big deal to us Romans, those priests acted as if it were the worst crime possible. Still, the priests represented political power in Judaea, even more so than their so-called King Herod, better known as Antipas.

After the actual King Herod the Great died, his heirs struggled for his throne. Caesar Augustus divided Herod's kingdom into four parts, naming a tetrarch, a governor to rule over each division. The regions of Peraea, east of the Jordan River, and Galilee went to Herod Antipas, who fancied himself a king. Regardless of his title, he served at Emperor Tiberius' discretion.

Likewise, the priests served at Pilate's will. I was told that Joseph ben Caiaphas was the last high priest appointed by Pilate's predecessor, Valerius Gratus, who cycled through no less than six high priests during his tenure as prefect. Having learned by watching others fail, Caiaphas knew how to honor his Roman masters sufficiently to avoid getting the boot. That way, he could continue enjoying his priestly position's luxuries. Thus, Pilate allowed Caiaphas to stay. Still, the Jews had only the power we Romans allowed them to have.

When it was evident that the charge of blasphemy would not persuade Pilate, the priests accused the man of having claimed to be a king, though it was apparent he was of meager means and not a king. I had to stifle a laugh when Prefect Pilate mocked their demands to execute him by saying to Caiaphas, "Shall I crucify your King?"

Then as if they were engaged in verbal swordplay, Caiaphas said they had no king but Caesar. Maybe he thought he was tricking the prefect into action. But it was Pilate who had maneuvered that pious cult into pledging their sole allegiance to Caesar.

We all knew the Jews longed for the day a Messiah from their precious line of David would take the throne, thereby usurping Rome of its control. Saying *they had no king but Caesar* meant they had abandoned their Messiah. Or perhaps they were lying. Either way, their declaration motivated Pilate to order my uncle, Centurion Cassius Longinus, to add the battered man to our roster of prisoners to be crucified. When I heard that decision, my mouth gaped open with a pop. Uncle Cassius turned his eyes to me.

Well, it was only one eye. The other had been rendered unusable years ago, leaving behind a white mass of mangled tissue. Rumor had it that my uncle had fought as a gladiator years ago. Reportedly he had won his freedom after a victory in the Colosseum, impressing Tiberius, or maybe it had been Augustus. Either way, it was long ago. He didn't talk about it, at least not with any young legionaries, even if one of them was his nephew.

As a token of respect for the Jewish holiday, as was his practice, Pilate chose to release a prisoner after the Jews' annual Passover celebration. Allowing a condemned man to live was almost as good as executing him, or maybe better because it showed the locals that we Romans were in control. We all expected the scourged rabbi to be the one released. His reputation was one of feeding the hungry and healing the sick. Some people insisted they'd seen him bring the dead back to life.

Upon further investigation, Lazarus of Bethany, the resurrected person, turned out to be a close friend of the accused. So, whether it was sleight-of-hand or actual magic, it was of little consequence for Rome. Now, if this Rabbi had demonstrated a different kind of power over death, say if he could cause a cohort to drop dead—that would be serious. We'd have to deal decisively with anyone having that kind of power.

During his arrest the previous night, there had been some confusion. I was in the Roman cohort supporting the temple guards who arrested him. Pilate sent an entire cohort because the priests were convinced there'd be thousands of citizens around the foot of the Mount of Olives willing to fight for the rabbi. If true, it could have marked the beginning of a regional war against Rome. Naturally, we were all on edge.

After we assembled in battle formation at the garden, we soon discovered that we faced less than a dozen timid men, and only one of them had a sword. A spy from within the rabbi's circle of friends identified him, and the weirdest thing happened. We all fell to the ground.

Why? I didn't know. There was no strong wind to blow us over. And even though I felt no shaking, I suppose it could have been an earthquake. It was dark and noisy, which added to the confusion.

How nearly six hundred armored men, braced for battle, could all lose their footing at once remains a mystery to me. Even more interesting, none of us were injured.

We scrambled back to our feet and were again ready for a fight. But there wasn't one to be had, except for a brief exchange between a lone armed disciple and Malchus, the Captain of the temple guards. While we were distracted getting back to our feet, the disciple swung his sword at Malchus, who shouted that his ear had been cut off. Upon closer inspection, his skin wasn't even broken. Although the temple guards dressed like soldiers, they were not credible. They reminded me more of children pretending to be soldiers.

While this man claimed to be a king, he didn't have an army and told Pilate his kingdom was not of this world. Indeed, a kingdom not of this world could not be a threat to the Roman Empire. The world was all we wanted, and nothing in Judaea could stop us.

Already convicted and locked in our prison, Barabbas was a community organizer who had been stirring up trouble and inspiring the locals to defy our Roman rule. The rebellion was foolish, as no nation could withstand our military might. The wise choice would be for them to pay their taxes and get on with their lives. Barabbas was declared guilty of promoting open rebellion against Roman rule. During his arrest, a man had been killed, and the evidence incriminated Barabbas enough to condemn him to the cross. Pilate gave the Jews a choice between freeing this convicted criminal or the rabbi. Their decision was stultifying.

Barabbas walked away a free man, probably to start more trouble, but he was not so clever as to be able to elude us the next time he broke the law. Like a dog to its vomit, he would soon return to his insurrectionist ways, and then we would capture, try, and crucify him. At least we had two of his subordinate rebels, Gestas and Dismas, in custody.

They showed the distress of their capture. Gestas was missing no less than six of his front teeth due to his foolish resistance to the soldiers who had apprehended him. Dismas had fared better with only a shallow wound on his bald head because he wisely surrendered when cornered.

During the riot, we'd caught them trying to steal Roman weapons. While the Romans had plenty of weapons, we didn't want the locals to think they had the right to bear arms. Once people can defend themselves, they might believe they don't have to worship Caesar or obey all of the laws he might decree. So, for the good of the Empire, Gestas and Dismas would have to die.

This Jewish festival season brought many surprises. The convicted insurrectionist Barabbas got out of jail and went free. The teacher, who did compassionate things for the locals but irritated the priests, got scourged and condemned to death. Caiaphas and his band of priests had arrogant smiles of victory. But, to their dismay, Pilate scrawled a sign identifying the rabbi as JESUS OF NAZARETH, THE KING OF THE JEWS, in Latin, Greek, and Hebrew, so all could understand it.

Caiaphas's eyebrows lifted, his body shook, and his head popped back, lifting his curly beard upward. He paused for a moment, as if stifling an angry scream, and through tight lips said, "Write not the King of the Jews, but that he said, I am King of the Jews."

Pilate wasn't one to take orders from people who worked for him. With a wave of his hand, he said, "Quod scripsi, scripsi."

What I have written, I have written.

We didn't get far. The beam was heavy, maybe a hundred pounds, and Jesus' body was mauled. I'd never seen a living man in a worse condition. His bloody legs buckled, and several men from the streets lunged forward as if they were going to strike him. I feared Jesus would be dead before we could nail his body to the cross if we allowed it. So, my fellow legionaries and I blocked their paths, striking some of them with our shields.

To these sheep herders, a shield appears to be a defensive tool. But, on the contrary, a Roman soldier is trained to use his scutum offensively nearly as much as it protected him from enemy weapons. During our basic training, we learned shield mastery by striking trees. Our Centurion could hear whether or not we were putting enough back into the strikes. He'd let us feel his energy if we didn't.

"Hit them like this!" He would correct us, telling us it was in our best interest. Train hard, fight easy, was as detailed as any explanation we'd ever get.

There can be little doubt that trees are much sturdier than flesh and bone. So, when we struck these locals, their teeth rattled, and they lost their footing. They'd feel our spears or swords next if they didn't flee. As expected, they folded back into the crowd with no appetite for a second helping of hurt.

After we restored order, Uncle Cassius rode up on his chestnut mare.

"By the knees of Venus, get that man on his feet!"

"He's too weak to carry the cross," I answered. Cassius rolled his eye and surveyed the crowd. A stout man, obviously Jewish but dressed in the fabric of the Cyrenians, stood between two young boys.

"You, there." Cassius pointed at him. "What's your name?"

"I am Simon. I'm a pilgrim from Cyrene, here for the festival with my two sons."

"Simon, you will carry this man's cross."

7

"But I must look after my boys." He put his arms around the youngsters.

Cassius glared down at them, his brow pulled low, and his lips pressed thin. "They're fine young lads. They can follow at a distance, and we'll release you at Golgotha. It's just past the gate. I won't ask you again."

Before he could answer, Cassius added, "Simon, do as I say, or, by Jupiter's beard, your sons will be carrying *your* body to its grave."

Simon opened his mouth as if he had an additional excuse to avoid the task. But after Cassius put his hand on the hilt of his sword, the reluctant Cyrenian pilgrim quickly obeyed.

Outside the eastern wall of Jerusalem was an overworked quarry used to deposit detritus and other garbage. In the middle was a sizable mound left unquarried because of its poor-quality stone. The locals called it Golgotha, which means *skull*. Despite the smell of death and the buzzing insects feasting on the rot, it was the perfect place for crucifixions.

As I rubbed my distressing nose, one of the nasty bugs flew at my face. After swatting it away, I imagined Hades must be much like Golgotha.

Except for the straightforward approach from the south, the steep sides made it simple for a few legionaries to defend it from unruly mobs seeking to speed up the death process. Because a standard crucifixion takes about four days to complete, it provides a deterrence to bad behavior.

We'd nail them to the beam and hoist them into position quickly, but then we had to wait. The boldest of criminals would sometimes bait us to run them through, to hasten their death and end their misery. Doing so would earn the foolish legionary either a beating from his Centurion or a session with the flagellum. If provoked almost to action, the wise legionary would request his Centurion's permission to break a few of the villain's toes but not the legs. Routinely, the leg breaking was performed on the third day, leading to death. Then the fourth day was for the birds and dogs to pick and gnaw, disfiguring the bodies well enough to dissuade anyone from repeating the dead guy's folly.

In Jerusalem, the priests forbade dogs and chickens oddly enough; however, with Golgotha outside the city walls, enough stray dogs were wandering about to do the job. Since people rarely claimed the mangled bodies, we'd put a hook in the carcasses, cut the ropes, yank them off the cross, and then drag them away for disposal.

Taking the better part of a week, legionaries were relieved by fresh troops from time to time. During those long waits, we appreciated having a view. The elevated position at Golgotha gave us a good observation point of the entire city, especially its majestic temple.

Supposedly, the God of the Jews lived in a room there behind a massive veil. Rumored to be a Babylonian curtain embroidered with blue, scarlet, and purple fine linen, it was something like sixty feet high, thirty feet wide, and as thick as a man's hand. I reasoned they thought they needed that much material to keep their God trapped there. The temple was between the Antonia Fortress to the north and the Royal Stoa to the south. In that place was where all the commerce and money changing happened.

Thousands of Jewish tombs were dug out of the remaining stone along the walls of the ancient quarry. But, of course, after our condemned criminals finally died, a peaceful tomb wasn't waiting for them unless they had family or friends to claim them. Instead, we usually tossed their lifeless bodies along with their crossbeams over the sides of the mound. There, they'd feed the worms as their final contribution to the world. Maybe all those skulls at the base of Golgotha helped explain its name.

I imagined that someday I might be asked to explain this remote place to my friends and family back in Rome. Should I survive until that day, I'd skip all those Hebrew words. This place would be called Calvaria in Latin, assuming anybody would be interested in it. Even young soldiers like me hope our service will make a difference for our families back home. My greatest fear wasn't dying in battle. Mostly, I didn't want my life wasted on useless things. Hopefully, crucifying the enemies of Rome would lead to a better world for all people. If they stopped resisting, they would discover that the peace Rome offered to all humanity was worth the taxes we required.

Someday, maybe we could forget about the sting and stink of death. Perhaps the peace at the end of this phase of humanity's progress will be so sweet that all of these events will fade into obscurity. I imagined all soldiers dreamt of peace.

***

At the third hour (roughly 9:00 in the morning), we hoisted Jesus up on his cross. With a stubby nail, we affixed Pilate's sign over his head. Jesus responded only with silence to our roughness and the storm of taunts from the locals, wagging their heads and saying, "Ah, you who destroys the temple and rebuilds it in three days, save yourself and come down from the cross."

Mobs can be cruel. Scoundrels often take advantage of the chaos to hurt others. This day, I found it particularly ludicrous how the well-dressed priests, supposedly honorable men, and their scribes, alleged to be intellectuals, were the worst tormentors. Since Caiaphas was nowhere in sight, I imagined he was relaxing in his ornate temple. Undoubtedly, he'd probably sent his junior priests to heap insults on the suffering Jesus for his final hours of life.

"He saved others, but he cannot save himself!"

"Let Christ, the King of Israel, descend now from the cross."

"Yes, let us see and believe."

Cassius was concerned that someone in the mob would pull a weapon from under those cloaks they wore, hoping to kill our prisoners before the crucifixions took place. As a law enforcement unit, we were assigned the task of making sure that death should come from a combination of exhaustion and asphyxiation. It was supposed to be a lesson to everyone who watched this so-called justice run its course. I looked back at the man in the middle and wondered what lesson his death would give the world.

Weary of constantly watching the mouthy priests, Uncle Cassius ordered us to clear away the locals from the rocky knoll. Enthusiastically springing to the task, we hoped they would attempt to stand their ground, but they had no spine for a fight. We moved forward as they retreated toward the city walls. After we'd gone far enough, we turned back.

"Best you stay far away," I warned the crowd as I returned to the summit. "Any of us can easily put a spear through your belly from fifty paces out." They sneered while complying. Such a distance would be challenging, requiring a certain degree of luck for any spearman, but I knew they didn't know that.

On the eastern side of the summit of Golgotha, I noticed a line of brightly colored shrubs contrasting against the sandy dust we kicked up with each step taken. To our north and south, the picked-over quarry had no other light violet, pinkish flowers. On closer inspection, the quarry did not have any other dark green plants either. Further out, olive orchards and vineyards dominated the countryside, but the area inside the quarry was a putrid debris field.

I stepped closer to the shrubs and took pleasure from the

plants' complex scent, which hinted at minty overtones. The fragrance matched that of a familiar medicine used to help treat coughs. I thought it was called hyssop, but these plants were different. Hyssop was noted for its woody stems, but I'd never seen any with such long stiff reeds.

Being forced to stay some distance away, the priests and scribes had to weigh the damage they were doing to their vocal cords against what pain they were inflicting on the dying man. As the mob's bellowing faded away, Jesus cast his bloody eyes upward, and I finally heard him speak.

"Father, forgive them, for they know not what they do."

I couldn't be sure if he were forgiving his people, who were reviling him, or me and my legionaries for hoisting him up there. Indeed, we didn't cause him to be on that cross. As soldiers, we were merely following orders.

Since he wouldn't need it anymore, we all wanted his purple, blood-soaked robe. The traditional solution was to tear the fabric into four equal parts, but that cloak didn't have any seams, as it was woven from the top throughout its entire length and width.

Where did a man of obvious meager means acquire such an exquisite item?

"This is quality work," I said. "It would be a shame to tear it."

After a brief discussion, we agreed to draw lots for the entire piece. I never won in those games, but somehow, this time, I did. The robe was all mine. Nobody wanted his crown of thorns, so it stayed planted in his swollen, blood-oozing brow.

While Jesus remained quiet, the two rebels, Gestas and Dismas, moaned in agony. We knew they would all die eventually, but it was human nature to pity them. We offered the three condemned men some of our posca, wine vinegar, cut with water and spiced with gall and honey.

This drink was a favorite beverage among we legionaries because it was stimulating, though much cheaper than wine, while being healthier than the local water. After saturating sponges with the posca squeezed from our wineskin, we lifted the sponges on our spear tips to reach the mouths of the dying men on the crosses.

The two rebels sucked at them like a couple of piglets on a sow's teat, but the King of the Jews turned his head away, rejecting its somewhat pain-deadening power. I wondered if perhaps the potion was the only thing besides death that could offer him comfort.

As I lowered my spear, I heard the rebel Gestas taunt his King. Laboring to push the words from his nearly toothless mouth, he said, "If you be the Christ, save yourself and us."

Jesus said nothing, but Dismas, in a weak voice, fighting for breath, rebuked his partner, "Don't you fear God, considering you are in the same condemnation? We deserve it, but this man has done nothing wrong."

I liked hearing Dismas accept the consequences of his actions because it made me feel my job was making a difference in this world.

Gestas frowned at his bald friend but had no energy to argue. Dismas looked toward the man in the middle and forced the words, "Lord, remember me when you come into your kingdom."

"Verily I say unto you, today you shall be with me in paradise."

What manner of man is this?

He was crucified because his priests hated him. In his agony, he refused our painkiller. Still, Jesus forgave his tormentors and then promised paradise to a dying man. Amazingly, that promise brought Dismas more comfort than would have a belly full of posca.

Who is this Jesus?

Then an unexplainable thing happened. Even though it was midday, the sky darkened as if night were falling. I looked up, and though no clouds were visible, the sun had faded to a dim sphere and barely gave any light. As we fretted about the growing darkness, the man on the cross shouted so loudly that he startled me, causing me to wonder if we were under attack.

"Eli, Eli, lama sabachthani?"

Standing at a great distance, one of the priests found humor in Jesus' shouting and yelled, "Behold, he's calling for Elijah."

"Let it be," shouted the other priests. "Let us see whether Elijah will come and save him." The pious pack of them laughed, pointed, and jeered at Jesus.

Uncle Cassius scoffed. "The black-robed jackals are lying. It is obvious that this Jesus is speaking a blend of Aramaic and Hebrew."

I was proficient in Aramaic and Latin, but as far as Hebrew went, it was all Greek to me. I looked up at my uncle and said, "What did he mean?"

"It means, *My God, my God, why have you forsaken me,* and those jeerers know it. The ancient words are recorded in their sacred scroll and attributed to their legendary King David."

"Why did they say he was calling Elijah? Who is that? Is he some mercenary or bandit who might try to rescue him?"

Cassius rubbed his chin and looked up toward the sky. "Stephanus, to become a successful military leader, you must know your history."

"I do know my history."

"Then tell me how Rome was founded."

"By Romulus and Remus."

"Those are mere names." Cassius sneered at my answer. Apparently, I had failed to meet his expectations. "A leader needs to communicate precisely when quizzed on topics of importance. Tell me about the founding of Rome."

I looked at the ground. No hint of an answer was there, but my sandals were dusty. "I'm not sure I can. It was somewhere around 800 years ago, I think."

"That much is correct. Romulus and Remus were twin sons of the priestess Rhea and Mars, the god of war. Initially left to drown, the river god, Tibernus, put them both on Palatine Hill, where a wolf named Lupa nursed them, a woodpecker fed them, and a local shepherd eventually raised them as his sons. The boys were so competitive that Romulus eventually killed his brother. Then Romulus built a strong wall about Platine Hill and established the foundations of Ancient Rome. He named the city after himself, and we inherited our greatness from him."

"Thank you." I made a point to listen closely so that I could repeat it if ever quizzed again, as unbelievable as the story was. The gods may be real, but wolves don't have names, and even if one did, it would have slaughtered those baby boys. Besides, woodpeckers never share their food except with their own young. Still, I wondered how that fairytale was supposed to help me understand who Elijah was.

Cassius chuckled. "Understanding your own story helps you understand the story of our competitors. Before Romulus and Remus were born, Elijah was a supernatural prophet, a champion of the Hebrew God."

"That was long ago."

"Absolutely. He ran faster than a speeding chariot, was more powerful than a cohort of Baal prophets, and was able to call down fire from the heavens."

"Super indeed." I marveled at the report. The Jews could make up stories as well as the Romans.

"He stopped the rain from falling for three and a half years, poured oil from a small jug that never ran dry, and raised a widow's son from the dead. King Ahab of Judah allowed his controlling wife, Jezebel, to slaughter the people who believed in Yahweh. After their God had enough of that, He sent Elijah to stop them."

"That's impressive. But having lived so long ago, even before

Rome's founding, he's certainly dead by now. How could a dead man rescue Jesus?"

"That's more of his supernatural story. He didn't die. His God sent a chariot of fire, with horses of fire, that took the still-living Elijah into heaven by a whirlwind."

"Really?" *He didn't die.* That's quite a plot twist.

"It's in their sacred scrolls. I don't think they'd lie to themselves."

"Assuming that Elijah has been living in heaven with his God all this time, why would he come back?"

"During the early Roman republic days, while we were still consolidating the cities in the middle of the Italian peninsula, over 400 years ago, another prophet in this part of the world, named Malachi, said that their God would send Elijah to change the people's hearts before the great and dreadful day of the Lord."

"Day of the Lord—what does that mean?"

"I don't know." Uncle Cassius scowled at the priests in the distance. "But the man on the cross wasn't calling Elijah. He was calling to his God, or at least repeating the words of their ancient king about being forsaken."

I had so many questions but didn't say them aloud. Was *being forsaken* a reference to the darkness? Was this dying man saying the gods were at play here? If so, which ones? Perhaps Elijah, as he sounded as powerful as most of the gods I was familiar with. Maybe Apollo? Or Jupiter? Could it be Yahweh, the God of the Jews, which I didn't know much about? Looking toward the city's temple, which was already lit with torches, I looked for clues. The only possible explanation was that supernatural powers were behind this strange darkness.

Was some spiritual battle happening, unseen by the rest of us?

I wondered how Jesus, being so near to death, could find enough air to shout. Of all the crucifixions I'd attended, merely speaking required a tremendous effort.

My Uncle Cassius sent two soldiers to the fortress to bring back torches. Soon the sun completely vanished, and strangely there was no moon or visible stars. It was not night, but it was dark. Within minutes, only the torches from Jerusalem provided any light. By then, the shouting crowds had retreated to the city, and a mysterious gloom filled the air, which was as still as if it were a dream.

———

Even though we had a perimeter lit by our torches, Cassius insisted we remain more vigilant than ever. Was he expecting an attack? If this were some kind of a trap, I wondered how they, whoever they were, had arranged it.

Who has the power to blot out the sun?

I'd seen the moon drift across the sun before, but neither of those heavenly bodies was anywhere to be seen. It felt as if we had been buried by night. Maybe the entire world had been swallowed by one of the gods. Perhaps the gods were at war.

Hoping my uncle could give me some insight, I asked, "Cassius, have you ever seen such darkness?"

"Never during the day," he said from atop his horse. "I don't know what to make of it. Sometimes during a dust storm, it can get dark."

"But there's not even a hint of a breeze in the air."

"True," Cassius agreed with me. "You can't have a dust storm without wind, plus there is no dust. This is baffling."

"Could it be that this Jesus is the man they say he is? Is he the Christ? The Messiah?"

"Do you even know what that means?" Cassius turned his head toward me as the torchlight cast an eerie glow across his helmet.

"That he is their King?" I said, "A god? The God?"

Cassius frowned. I waited, expecting a lecture about the

dangers of letting Jewish theology sway my beliefs. Instead, he said, "The Jews have prophets from centuries ago that testified a descendant of their revered King David would deliver his people."

"Deliver them from what? Rome?"

He shook his head. "The Jews have been conquered by every empire that's come along. They were slaves in Egypt and captives in Babylon, Assyria, and Persia. Oh, they had short periods of freedom but always returned to captivity or the rule of foreigners, just as Rome rules them today. Yet, despite being beaten, they hold on to their faith in the promised Christ. He's just never shown up. At least not that they've noticed."

"What about him?" I pointed at Jesus on the cross. "He had thousands of Jews following him around earlier, shouting *hosanna*. My Hebrew is weak at best, but I think that means, *Pray, save us*."

"It does, but where are they now?" Cassius held out his arms and twisted at his waist in his saddle. He shrugged and said, "Perhaps they are cowering in the darkness. Following a man for healing and free food or wanting to see the next magic trick isn't believing in him. They didn't even stand up for him at Gethsemane, not that it would have done much good. We were ready for them, but there was no resistance. At least none that made a difference."

"What if this darkness is some sort of preparation? What if he's about to come off that cross and get down to the business of delivering his people? What happens then?"

"Then, by the biceps of Mars, we'll put him back up there," said Cassius as he bowed up, ready to fight the next battle should it come. "Or die trying."

"I suppose, but how do we know he's not the real thing?"

"Time will tell all. Is he greater than our divine Emperor Tiberius? Our emperor lives, but this Jesus is about to die." Disturbingly the torchlight danced around Jesus' mauled body as if demons were taunting him about his imminent death. "Ask me after he's dead."

"Some have said he will rise on the third day after his death. Can any man do that? Do you think he has real power?"

"Real power produces freedom. I won my freedom in the arena, but it cost me an eye. That was nearly ten years ago." Cassius turned toward the man on the cross, paused for a few seconds, and then declared, "If Jesus heals my eye, I'll believe."

"Really?"

Cassius chuckled and said, "Sure, but he's got a better chance of rising from the grave than he does of doing that." Then Jesus cast a glance toward my uncle. A chill ran up my spine. I swallowed hard and assumed the darkness must have brought some cold with it.

Further back, the two rebels groaned. The pitch-black darkness made their lamentations even more miserable. To breathe, they pushed up with their feet to allow air to enter their lungs. Eventually, they'd have no strength to continue pushing. Ultimately, they'd die, but before that happened, they'd cry like hungry children.

The light from a couple of torches approached. I tightened the grip on my spear and wondered if this could be the attack Cassius was wary of. As they drew closer, I saw them in the glow of our torches. It was merely a band of women and a man a little older than me. He was thin but taller than the women.

Uncle Cassius, atop his horse, asked about their business with the dying men. As I'd been taught by my Centurion, I looked for any tell-tell signs of hidden weapons like a dagger's handle pressing against the inside of their cloaks but saw nothing. With a nod of his helmet, Cassius had us search their packages. Their parcels contained only a small vessel of wine and some spices, which smelled woody, warm, and medicinal. Was that myrrh or something else? Either way, it wasn't a weapon.

One of them was his aunt, another his mother, Mary, and some other women, all named Mary except for one called Salome. The young man said his name was John. I was sure I'd seen him with Jesus earlier, but his confidence was unusual, unlike the other followers who had fled. This unarmed man appeared to have no fear. So, I assumed I'd been mistaken. Even though they seemed harmless, I closely watched their movements as we allowed them to approach the cross in the middle for their little family reunion.

Most of them called him Yeshua, but his mother called him Jesus, like the name on the sign over his head. His aunt spoke not, as she couldn't stop crying.

"Woman, behold thy son." Jesus turned to John and said, "Behold thy mother."

Mary and John looked at each other for a few moments, and Jesus said, "I thirst."

One of the Marys mixed some of their myrrh into the container of wine. I knew there was no way they could get the jug up to Jesus' mouth, so I offered a sponge on the tip of my spear. I thought they would dip the sponge in the wine. Instead, one of the women pulled the sponge off my spear as John yanked a stiff reed from those wispy branches in the row of hyssop. Then Jesus' mother put the sponge on the reed, and John lifted it to Jesus' mouth for a sip.

With a voice as strong as any Roman Centurion bellowing orders to his men, Jesus shouted, "It is finished." He looked upward and said, "Father, into your hands, I commit my spirit."

A whirlwind swirled up from the ground as a blinding flash exploded to the west of us. The noise was louder than a blacksmith's hammer on hot iron. My shoulders pushed upward as if trying to touch my ears. Then another bolt of lightning struck to the north of us. With it came a surge of sunlight from the sky. And another. And then four more deafening energy bolts slammed downward, dancing around Golgotha. When the horrific lightning storm ended, the sun blazed again in the sky. The ground shook with violent energy, splitting rocks into pieces. The trash-filled quarry roiled as if it were boiling water. We all fell to our knees. In the distance, people screamed, and parts of the city wall fell to the ground—the sound of a thousand tunics being torn at once came from the direction of the temple. The famous colossal veil there had been torn from top to bottom. Smoke billowed upward as fire licked at the temple's base. Looking south, I saw many people wearing burial clothes, calmly emerging from the tombs.

Out of the tombs?

My mind was flooded with questions. Why were they there? Was it their refuge during the dark? Why did they hide in the tombs instead of the buildings in the city? Why were they dressed like the dead? And why hadn't I noticed them earlier? Perhaps the darkness had covered their movement. The Jews are a strange people. I wasn't sure if I would ever understand them.

Dust and sand were whirling through the valley, tossed about by the wind, which added to our distress. The sand stung my face, causing me to lift my free hand to protect my eyes. Grit invaded my teeth, and the dryness caused my tongue to cleave to the roof of my mouth. I reached for the wineskin, hoping to quench my thirst when I noticed we had distinguished company coming our way, so I refrained.

Two Roman cavalry officers rushed toward us from the direction of Herod's Palace south of us. Desiring a swish of posca, I hoped their visit would be short. Cornelius, the Centurion of Pilate's Italian cohort, dismounted and walked toward Cassius. Cornelius carried two sledgehammers.

With a nod, Cornelius said, "The Prefect has ordered the crucifixions to be expedited."

"By the winged feet of Mercury, what's the rush?" asked Cassius as he dismounted to face him as an equal.

"The Jewish sabbath," Cornelius replied as he offered one of the sledgehammers to my uncle. "The priests obtained Herod's support to convince Pilate to order the bodies taken off the cross before their sabbath. It has something to do with their religious tradition. Pilate ordered that we make sure they're dead first. So, we must break their legs."

Cassius took both hammers and gave one to me and the other to one of my fellow legionaries. Then, after laying our spears down, we went to work on the wretched rebels.

Breaking their legs prevented them from pushing up; therefore, they'd not be able to breathe. In a way, it was more merciful as they'd die in minutes instead of days. Still, breaking a man's legs with a sledgehammer was gruesome for the doers like me and most painful for the crucified like toothless Gestas and Dismas. Under the trauma of our blows, both men sounded more like animals than people. During my limited experience in the military, I learned that most men don't die stoically like soldiers are supposed to. As far as that goes, neither do most soldiers.

Bloody hammer in hand, I stepped toward Jesus. Then I stopped. Pale skin, blue lips, no body movement—he was a corpse. I paused long enough to inspire Cornelius to shout at me from behind.

"What are you waiting for? Strike!"

"He's gone." I shrugged. "You want I should break a dead man's legs?"

Uncle Cassius moved closer, picked up my spear from the ground, and said, "Maybe he's merely passed out. But, if he's dead, this won't hurt him a bit."

Burly uncle Cassius thrust my spear upward through Jesus' side so far that it had to have pierced his heart. Then Cassius yelled and trembled as if he'd been hit by lightning. Grunting and jerking, Cassius finally pulled the spear back to him. After an unexplainable flash, a deluge of carmine blood and water gushed out of Jesus as if he were a fountain. The spray covered my uncle's face. Perhaps the wind carried it because the blood also sprayed my shoulder plates, helmet, and face. Much of it even got onto Cornelius.

How could one man have enough blood to cover us all?

Cassius dropped my spear and used both hands to vigorously wipe the blood away as if panicked. Finally, he spoke, but his words sounded like gibberish.

I felt the hairs on the back of my neck stand on end, and then the same tingling sensation rushed down my arms and legs. My fingers and toes became hypersensitive, and my lingering thirst left me. Everywhere this man's blood had sprayed gave off a faint warm glimmer. A light flashed, and instantly, where there had been no one, a man was standing in front of me.

His face glowed, and his cloak glistened like fresh snow on the Italian alps. A bright cloud overshadowed him, which spoke.

"This is my beloved Son, in whom I am well pleased. Listen to him."

The glowing man's eyes locked onto mine. Then, in perfect Latin, with the comfortable dialect of my youth, he said, "Stephanus, if you seek me and believe in me, I will save you."

His voice was familiar. I knew I had seen him before. His hair and complexion were perfect, with features more than handsome; this man was beautiful. Then I knew.

"You're Jesus." My head swirled as if I'd had too much posca. But in the place of the incoherent thoughts of a drunken man, my life flashed before me. It was more ordered, with less chance than I had remembered. Somehow Jesus had been in my life all along, and on at least two occasions, he or his angels had prevented my death. I lost any confidence I'd ever had in the Roman gods and doubted my unbelief in this person called Jesus until a strange thought came to my mind.

If only you were Jewish, you could follow him, but you're not.

"Everyone who calls on my name will be saved," Jesus answered my doubt, but I was torn between self and duty.

Obviously, he had escaped the cross. What to do? As a Roman soldier, I defaulted to my duty to Rome. The words of Cassius echoed in my mind, telling me to put him back on the cross or die trying. The hammer fell from my hand as I scanned the ground for my missing spear. Beyond the glow streaming from Jesus, there was a hazy bubble as if I were underwater. In the distance, I saw the outlines of Cassius and Cornelius, but I wasn't sure if they were really them.

Was I dreaming?

"This is no dream, Stephanus. You can't put me back on the cross. Behold, my body is still there."

Then with a snap, the glow vanished, as did the vision of Jesus, and I became aware of Golgotha's sights, sounds, and smells of death. Three dead men on crosses cast shadows over the other soldiers and me. I spun around, expecting to see the departing vision, but it was gone without a trace.

What manner of witchery is this?

Concerned that I might have been poisoned by either the blood or the posca, I wondered if I was going out of my mind. I rubbed the blood away from my mouth with my newly acquired robe. Then I stepped closer to Cornelius, hoping for some of his sage leadership, but he didn't even look at me. Instead, the two of us stood there frozen, watching Cassius stagger about with his mouth gaped open. He held first one hand to cover his left eye, then the other hand over his right eye. Jerking his head backward, he looked up to the sky, where the sun was shining, and laughed out loud. He seemed to be talking to someone that we could not see.

Has he gone insane, or perhaps he has also been poisoned?

Cassius took a deep breath and slowly let it out before looking at Cornelius, who by then had dropped to his knees and had tears running down his cheeks. Then my uncle's eyes locked onto mine. They surprised me as they were like two black cherries under his thick salt-and-pepper eyebrows.

"Your eye!"

No longer a bleached plug of useless flesh, it was perfect. I reached out, but he slapped my hand away as if it were an annoying insect. At first, my hand stung from the sharp blow, but then it went numb. The numbness spread throughout my body as I struggled to regain my composure. Sweat ran down my brow, and my knees knocked together as I fought against the shadows of the thoughts surging through my consciousness.

Cassius turned his gaze to Jesus, still hanging on the cross behind me. Moving closer, my uncle embraced the feet of the dead man and said, "Truly, this man was the Son of God."

GENERATIONAL CURSE

PRISCILLA ADAMS

*B*illy grabs his coffee cup and adds six spoons of sugar, then gets his iPad and sits by the window, watching the sunrise. It's 6 a.m., but he's used to early mornings, and once he has his coffee, he is ready for the day. Growing up in Texas, in the country, he woke up so early that sometimes he'd beat the sun up. He's already run a brush through his long blond hair, shaved, and dressed for work in jeans and a green polo shirt that Debra says matches his eyes. In fact, she had bought him this shirt and a few more in the same color. Billy, not being big on style, couldn't care less if the color matched his eyes. Debra was just the opposite; she loved fashion, style, and color. Since he was seeing her later and loved to see her smile, he put on the shirt. Billy knew he was decent looking, but he was no Maurice Benard, but Debra was gorgeous. How did a rugged country boy like him get a woman like that? She had the type of beauty that made men look twice, a slender, curvy figure that other women wished they had. Best of all, she was down-to-earth, kind, God-fearing, and patient.

Billy looks at the time on his iPad. Debra should be up now and ready to do their morning Bible Study. A seven-day plan on hearing God. An idea that she got from his mother, who adored Debra. He sips his coffee and waits for her call. He will have to leave for work in half an hour, and even though his family owns the company, he doesn't like to take advantage of it. James, his older brother, works with him in the company, and he is expecting Billy for a 7:30 meeting. Since it's after 6:30, he may have to call Debra. Hopefully, she's awake and didn't hit the snooze button over and over. Just then, his iPad rings. He sees her beautiful heart-shaped face, smooth brown skin, warm dark eyes, and he smiles.

"Hey, Beautiful. I was beginning to think that you just kept hitting the snooze button this morning, and I was going to have to call and wake you up."

"Hey, yourself, Handsome. I won't lie, I did hit the snooze a few times, but I eventually got up. Just a little later than usual. So, what's your day look like?"

"I've got a meeting with James Jr. this morning, and then we're going out to one of the job sites. I will see you later over here for family dinner, right?"

"Absolutely, babe. So let's get into this plan."

Debra pulls up to Billy's house, and judging from all the luxury cars parked, it seems most of his family has already arrived. Billy's grandfather started the family business over fifty years ago, then Billy's father took over when he retired. James Jr. being the oldest, is in line to take over when their Dad retires later this year.

Getting out of the car, Debra is looking forward to seeing Billy's family. Being raised in foster care and not having a family of her own, makes being welcomed and accepted by Billy's family a blessing. Even though she and Billy have only been dating for three months, she's formed bonds with his family, and the feeling seems mutual.

Debra knocks at the front door, then opens it and goes in. Billy's parents are sitting on the couch; his brother James, his wife Jessica, and their two kids are there, along with Melanie, Billy's younger sister. Debra spots Billy coming out of the bedroom.

"Hey, Deb! What's good, Mama?" Melanie comes over and gives her a big hug. She's a free spirit, today sporting blue hair extensions that make a bold statement against her blonde hair. Other than the family's trademark blonde hair, she's nothing like her brothers.

Hugging her back and smiling. "Hey, girlie. I'm doing great. It's good to see you! Where've you been?"

"Some friends invited me to Canada, so I hopped on a flight and got outta town for a while."

Jessica comes over and puts her arms around both of them. "Hi ladies, come on in and get a drink with me."

"Let me go speak to Mr. and Mrs. Houston first." Debra goes over to hug both of Billy's parents and say hello. Billy comes up behind her and grabs her hand, pulling her in for a hug and quick kiss.

"Hey, fam, can I get your attention?" He holds his hands up, and the kids quiet down. "We're going to eat dinner in a minute, but I want to do something first. Follow me." They all walk out to the huge backyard. The pool is lit up, and dangling lights surround the patio decorated with colorful flowers. Everyone is amazed at how beautiful it is. As they come out, a violinist starts to play, and the band joins in. Then to their surprise, Faith Hill and Tim McGraw enter singing *I Need You.* Debra is shocked. She smiles at Billy as they listen to the duet. Once the song ends, Billy gets down on one knee in front of her with a beautiful ruby ring in his hand.

She gasps and looks at him questioningly. What is he doing? Is he really doing this? Already? What will she say?

"Debra, you know I love you. We haven't known each other long, but my soul knew you long before we met face to face. These last three months have been the brightest of my life because you light up my life. I'm not the smartest man, but I know my life is better with you by my side, and I want it to always be that way. Will you marry me and be my wife?"

This was really happening! He was proposing, here in front of everybody. Debra's heart was beating so loud she could hardly hear, but she could feel a huge smile spreading all over her face, matching the joy in her heart.

"Yes, Baby, I will marry you!" He slips the large princess-cut ruby ring on her finger. She reaches up and throws her arms around his neck, and he leans down and kisses her. They look up to see the family looking at each other hesitantly, then back at them. There's a moment of awkward silence. The band plays again, James starts to clap, and the others join in. Melanie just shakes her head and walks back in.

Debra is still reeling from the proposal a few nights ago as she tries to focus on the article that she's writing for the magazine. Wow! Faith Hill and Tim McGraw sang just for them. If Billy arranged for them to sing at his surprise proposal, there's no telling whom he would get to sing at their wedding. Six months should be enough time to plan their wedding. She didn't have any family, just her bestie Deanna, who seemed less enthusiastic about her engagement, and a few friends from college and work. Billy's list, on the other hand, would be long since he had a large family. Where would they get married, and when? They needed to set a date.

LouAnn Houston sits on the couch with her husband, James Sr., in the huge living room of their family home they shared with Billy and Melanie. Billy isn't there yet, and for a good reason. She wants to talk with everyone before he arrives so they will all be on the same page. She sighs as she looks at James, knowing he is reluctant to have this conversation with his younger brother because he's always been his protector. They've been inseparable most of their lives. He knows the issues his brother struggles with better than anyone except maybe Melanie.

"This proposal of your brother's has your father and me worried. We think Debra is wonderful, but they've only known each other for three months, and she doesn't know your brother as well as she thinks she does."

Melanie is a bit more direct. "You mean she doesn't know about his crazy mood swings, being charged up, super excited, sometimes rude and aggressive, then falling into weeks of depression? I'm sorry, but I can't be happy for them. Deb's fantastic, but she has no idea what she's getting herself into."

James Sr. says, "It's not his fault; he has a condition. He tries to control it. Sometimes he just needs time to himself. He's handling it."

Lou Ann sighs, "I wonder if he's going into a manic phase. I'm also worried about how he'll react when Debra sees this side of him. Will she reject him, or will she try to support him? It's a lot for her to take on, especially if he's not honest with her. Hiding it can't be good for him or her."

"Mama, he doesn't believe anything is wrong with him. That's why he won't get treated and why his relationships always come to an abrupt end. If I weren't his sister, I wouldn't put up with him either, and that's why I keep my distance."

"You two used to be so close. I don't like seeing how far apart you are now."

James Jr. chimes in. "Billy is ok. He really loves Debra, and wants to marry her. Society would have you thinking it takes a long time to know you love someone, but that's not true. You'll know almost immediately. When you know why wait? Besides, I'll be there to help him if I see him going off the deep end. *We'll* be there for him. That's what family is for."

"Frankly, Jr., you're enabling him. I know you want to protect him, but you can't protect him from himself. When he gets here, we need to all be on the same page."

"And what page is that?"

"We need to encourage him to take some time and think through this engagement and take some more time to get to know Debra and for her to get to know him. The good and the bad. He needs to tell her about his bipolar disorder."

"I don't know; maybe he should tell her when he's ready. As far as their engagement, I think she's great for him. She's great, period, and by the time the wedding happens, they will know each other much better."

They hear Billy come in the front door. Lou Ann sits up straight and nods and catches Melanie's eye and sees that she's fidgeting with the bracelet on her wrist, so she smiles at her as if to assure her that everything will be fine.

"Hey there, Son. How are you doing today?"

"Hey, Dad. I'm having a pretty swell day. We got that contract for the oil rigs with that new company I was working on."

"Whoa, way to go, Bro! Good work." James Jr. smiles at him, hoping it will make him more at ease.

Billy looks around at everyone. "So what's this family meeting about?"

The room is silent, and finally, James Sr. speaks up. "Son, we were all stunned when you proposed to Debra at dinner the other night. It seems a bit sudden, and a man ought to take his time with something like this. The woman ought to as well."

Billy looks at each of their faces. So, this is why they're having a family meeting, because they don't want him to marry Debra.

"Dad, you all seem to get on great with Debra. Y'all have told me how good she is for me, so what's changed?"

His mother speaks up, in a calm, quiet tone. "Nothing, Billy. It's just that we think you should take more time to get to know each other, the good, the bad, and everything in between. That takes time."

"I don't need any more time. I love Debra, and I'm happy with her. What else is there to know?"

"But does she know all there is to know about you?" Mel cautiously asks.

"What are you getting at?" Billy starts to see where this meeting is going, and the heat rising up in him makes him clench his teeth.

Melanie speaks up. "Sometimes your mood turns really dark, and you get angry about the smallest things; then you apologize, but a couple months later, it's the same thing. I'm tired of the roller coaster ride. Eventually, Deb will be too."

James Jr. attempts to diffuse the situation by explaining, "We're just concerned that you may be getting overly hyper like you sometimes do and jump the gun on things without thinking them through. You sometimes have some depression or anger, and maybe Debra hasn't been with you long enough to know how to handle that."

Billy starts pacing. "So you feel this way too? You think I need to slow things down with Debra because what? She hasn't been with me long enough to realize I'm crazy!! And you think I don't know what I'm doing just because I know what I want, and I'm not going to waste years of our lives getting to know each other."

James Sr. goes to put a hand on his son's arm. "No one is saying you're crazy, son. We know you're not. Just calm down; we're only trying to help."

Baby, you know you have bipolar disorder. Just because you think you're managing it doesn't make it go away. Trust me, I know. Debra may not be able to handle that. You need to tell her. You should have told her before you proposed. What if she isn't willing to be with you when you go through your mood swings or episodes?" LouAnn keeps her tone calm but refuses to sugarcoat the situation. Best to tell him like it is so that he can face it and realize he needs to deal with it.

"Debra loves me. She's not going to leave me because of a few ups and downs. I don't need to tell her anything! I have it under control, and it's going to stay that way. I am not taking any chances on losing her. So, you can dislike it all you want. I'm not changing my mind."

"Son, you don't have to."

Melanie looks at her brother, sees his anger, and she knows there's no more reasoning with him. "Daddy, just let it go."

"Yes, let it go, " Billy says sarcastically to Melanie. "I couldn't have said it better, little sis. I'm leaving, and you all can continue talking about me behind my back..." Billy walks out, slamming the front door.

Debra smiles as she sees Billy waving at her from the table in the crowded deli. She was surprised by his impromptu call asking to have lunch with him. Usually, he's so busy at work or out on location they hardly get to go to lunch together. He stands up, leans over, and kisses her as she gets ready to sit down. They chit-chat while she looks over the menu to decide what to order. She's starving, and the giant baked potato with the Mexican fixings looks delicious.

"So, Sweetheart, I've been thinking about our wedding." Billy jumps right into his big announcement. "We need to make plans."

"Yeah, I was thinking we might want to start looking at dates, then we can search for the right venue, and once we—"

"I say we skip all that. Let's fly to Vegas and elope! We can book a suite at the Bellagio, get married right there with all the beautiful lights, and just spend the week honeymooning, 'or we can fly somewhere else to honeymoon. Whatever you want."

"Oh, I hadn't thought about eloping. I assumed you'd want a big wedding with all of your family and friends there."

"Nah. I just want you. I'm ready to start our life together, so let's book a flight. You pick the hotel, and we're there."

"Ok, let me check my schedule, and we can look at some times that work for us." Debra reaches over to get her phone out of her purse, but Billy stops her.

"No need, let's go today. I can book us a flight from my phone, and we can go pack a few things and be off. I'll check now to see if the Honeymoon Suite is available; any hotel you want."

"Billy, today? I have to finish this article for the magazine and submit it for editing. Besides, you can't just take off work!"

"I own the company. Of course I can."

"This is so sudden!"

"It's spontaneous! Isn't that good in a relationship?"

"Yeah, but…we don't even have wedding bands."

"Let's go shopping right now."

"Don't you have to get back?"

"James Jr. can handle the business.

"Ok, but—"

"But nothing. Let's do it!"

Debra opens her eyes and looks around the room. The suite they're in is beautiful and spacious, with a gorgeous view of the strip. Caesars Palace was everything she expected and more. She loved the art. The Greco-Roman culture was everywhere you went in the hotel. She smiled as she thought of their wedding ceremony.

Though it was not how she saw her wedding day, it was still beautiful. The hotel's chapel had large Roman sculptures, a beautiful fountain, and flowers all around. She looked down at her hand, and the ruby glowed against the sparkling diamonds of her wedding band. Just then, there was a knock at the door, and she could hear Billy in the living room letting in room service.

Billy sets up the breakfast on the table by the window and opens the drapes for Debra. As he turns, he sees her coming into the room.

"Good morning, Mrs. Houston. Come in and have breakfast."

"Morning, babe. Oh, my goodness, did you order everything they had? How much did this cost?"

"Well, I couldn't decide, and I wasn't sure what you would want, so..." Billy pulls out her chair, motioning for her to sit. "Come on, let's eat so we can get started on the rest of our honeymoon."

By the end of the week, Debra was utterly worn out. Billy was so hyper. He wanted to do everything there was to do in Vegas; walk the strip, see shows, and gamble. He was spending so much money at the tables that she had to pull him away. He'd even had the nerve to get mad at her and cause a scene in the casino. Billy was spending money like it was water, and though he was wealthy, it seemed wasteful. Luckily, he had won big, so that made up for some of the money he'd spent.

Now, they were on their way home. She would pack up some clothes and start moving into Billy's home. Over the next week, she would hire a moving company to pack up everything else and get it all moved for her. Billy was talking about some sports game, but Debra was so tired that she drifted off to sleep.

Billy is in his office catching up on work. There was a lot to do. He'd been gone a whole week. An *unplanned* week and things were all over the place. Before he knew it, the day was over, and it was time to go home, where Debra would be waiting for him. It was such a nice thought that they would start and end every day together. There was a knock at his door just as he was about to log off his desktop. He yelled, "Come in!" and was surprised and a little nervous when his Dad walked in.

"Hey, Dad, what are you doing here?"

His Dad walks in looking grim. "What do you think? You just up and left, leaving your brother to do his job and yours, with no heads up, nothing in place, nothing!"

"I know, and I'm sorry, but I've got great news!" Billy excitedly tells his Dad, dismissing his dad's anger.

"Yeah, I heard. You and Debra got married. You jetted her off to Vegas and left your brother and the crews in a lurch."

"Dad, I'm back now, and…"

"Come on. You're coming with me." His dad turns and walks back out of the office.

"What? Where are we going?"

"To see your Grandpa."

They arrive at an upscale nursing home. The grounds are beautiful, and the rooms are small yet nice. As they walk into his grandpa's room, the nursing assistant is reading to him. Billy sees him in bed propped up and swears his grandpa is looking at her breasts. James Sr. speaks to the assistant and asks how his dad is doing. She tells him that he's been very hyper for the last couple of weeks, even though he can't walk well, so they've had to watch him even more carefully than usual. Now he's melancholy and sleeping a lot.

"Hey, Pops, it's James. I come to visit ya, and look who I brought with me." He leans over so that his Dad can see him better.

Pops tears his eyes away from the nursing assistant and looks over to see his son and grandson. "Jamie, it's about time you got your ass out here to see me, and you brought my grandson. Get over here, Billy."

"Pops, I was just here two weeks ago. You don't remember? You're forgetting a lot more lately."

Billy goes over and sits by Pop's bed.

"Pops. How have you been?"

"As good as a lonely old man can be, I guess. Been kinda down lately, so it's good to see you. Tell me what's going on witcha."

James Sr. speaks up. "Pops, Billy here is a lot like you and me. He had great days where he felt on top of the world, life was exciting, and nothing and no one could touch him. But then there's also the low days, where he misses work because he's so depressed he doesn't want to leave the house."

"Dad, what do you mean, like y'all?"

"Son, I mean, I have the same struggles that you have and the same struggles my dad has." He looks at his dad lying in bed, who's looking at Billy with sad eyes.

"Dad, you have Bipolar? And Pops too?"

"Yes, son, and I put your mother through some tough times. My mania, the arguments, arrogance. There were so many times she put me out, and I begged my way back home. We always told you kids I was out of town for work, but I was in a motel, hoping she would forgive me, which she did. Then there was the depression. Sometimes I couldn't even leave the bedroom for days. She had to start stepping in and help Pops with the company until I could get myself back together."

"Things must have gotten better. You and Mom are still together. You must have been able to manage it."

"I thought I was, but it was hurting your mother and eventually took a toll on her. We're not as happy as we used to be, and truth be told, it's a big house, and we're more like roommates." He turns to his Pops. "Pops, tell him why Mom left you. See, Billy here just got married. Just took off and went to Vegas with Debra and didn't bother telling her about his condition."

Pops looks at Billy and pats his hand. "Boy, I was just like you. Didn't think nothing was wrong with me and so there was nothing to tell. Back then, we didn't have names for what was going on, but there was definitely something going on, and it drove your Granny away. I drove your Granny away. Worst mistake of my life. That's why I'm alone now. I don't blame her, though. Can't, because she tried, but it never stops, you see, not even in my old age."

James Sr. looks at his son. "I was the same as Pops here, but you don't have to be. There's a name for it, and there's medication for it now. You can have a different life with Debra, but you have to tell her first."

Pops grabs both of their hands, and there are tears in his eyes. "This is like a curse that I've suffered from and passed down to my son. And now he's passed it down to you. This has to stop, and you need to be the one to stop it."

James Sr. squeezes their hands. "I want us to pray, right now together, that this ends with you, son. That you have the heart and the strength to face this sickness and fight it. To get the help that you need and to be honest with Debra about it. I believe she loves you, but it's going to take more than that to stay with you through it all, so we'll pray for her too."

They bow their heads as James Sr. leads them in prayer.

Billy walks into his bedroom. Debra is putting up some clothes she brought over from her place. He hugs her from behind. She turns around and hugs him back. He's so nervous that he's shaking.

"Babe, what is wrong?" She looks up at him, concerned. It was such a change from the mood he's been in the past week. Maybe the family gave him a hard time about running off and getting married without telling anyone.

"Debra, I need to talk to you about something," he says nervously. He's so scared to reveal to her that he has a mental illness. What will she say? Will she be angry? Annul the marriage?

They sit down on the bed. Debra grabs his hands and rubs them as she waits for him to talk. He tells her about his mood swings, how his Mama took him to a psychiatrist in high school, and how he was diagnosed with Bipolar I Disorder. He explains that he's always felt like he could manage it on his own, and that he never even considered treatment or medication. Finding out his dad and grandfather both suffered from it was surprising, as well as how it hurt his mom and broke up his grandparents' marriage. It made him realize that if he wanted to have a healthy marriage with her, he needed to get help.

Debra looks at him, surprised by everything he is saying. She knew that this last week he was extremely hyper, energetic, and spontaneous, but she didn't realize these were all symptoms of a manic episode.

"Billy, I'm so sorry that you struggle with this. I had no idea."

"How could you? You've only known me a few months. I knew, and I should have told you, but I was so scared of losing you."

"I love you, Billy. I married you for better or worse, and I trust God."

Billy leans over and hugs her.

Debra pulls back. "Wait. Were you in a manic state when you proposed to me? Do you really even want to be married to me?"

She looks at him, wondering if her marriage is falling apart already and if he wants out.

"No, sweetheart, I absolutely want to be married to you. I was myself when I proposed to you, and I want to live my life with you, and I'm willing to do whatever I have to do to be well so we can be happy."

Debra smiles and hugs him. "Ok then. Well, let's get you some help."

———

Billy walks into the church with Debra, looking around curiously. He'd never been to a black church before. Following Debra nervously, he made his way to the front of the sanctuary, where a few people waited for them. Debra had asked him if he would like her pastor and the elders of the church to pray and lay hands on him. She said it would help heal him from the Bipolar. He'd never had it done before, but he believed in spiritual healing.

They placed him and Debra opposite of one another, face to face and holding hands while they surrounded them; each of them joining hands. Each one prayed over him for deliverance and healing. The elders prayed for their marriage, their future children, and generations to come. The pastor anointed them with oil and laid hands on them. It was such a moving experience. Everyone prayed with such passion, pleading to the Lord on his behalf. Speaking with such authority and conviction.

When they were done, it took a while before he could open his eyes. Debra was grasping one of his hands, and with the other, she was wiping tears from her eyes. He let her hand go and reached up to wipe the tears from his own.

———

Debra and Billy are in Dr. Tuley's office. He's an experienced psychiatrist that has been treating Billy's mom for years, helping her cope with her husband's Bipolar. Billy's very nervous, but Debra is with him so that they can find out what this journey will be like for them.

"I want to tell you that, yes, Bipolar I is a serious condition, and I commend you for taking the step to seek treatment. Both of you. I know it's scary, but the good news is that it is treatable, and the medications can help you stay well and not have more episodes. The key is finding the right dose, and Billy, you will need to continue to take your medication even when you feel great. There's hope."

Billy and Debra leave out of Dr. Tuley's office feeling very hopeful about their future. They look at each other and smile as they head toward the door, then stop to speak to a couple in the waiting room.

"Don't be nervous, Dad. Dr. Tuley is cool. There's hope for us." He leans down and kisses his mom on the cheek. "Things are going to get better, Mom, for all of us."

THE BACKUP BEAUTY QUEEN

JANN FRANKLIN

*L*ouisiana towns host more festivals than the calendar has days. We celebrate crawfish, meat pies, pirates, and boudin. We even recognize rougarous, the Cajun French version of a werewolf that lurks in the swamps.

Most of our festivals crown a queen during the celebration. These young ladies maintain high-grade point averages, cultivate memberships in multiple respected societies and clubs, and dream of lofty aspirations beyond high school. According to the Pirate Festival website, there isn't a Queen of the Pirates. Hopefully, her time is coming. I, for one, would enjoy wearing my Queen of the Pirates crown as I pushed my cart among the produce at my local grocery store. As would most of my fellow women folk. Who wouldn't want to sport a sash and tiara while sorting through melons and tomatoes? It is a prestigious honor to be the home of a festival queen, and our small village takes it seriously.

With high hopes, Graisseville had entered a contestant for the last decade, anticipating her success. Each time, the young lady returned with her head bare. Our village mantra became *next year.*

In the eleventh year, we actually believed it. That would be our triumph. That was the year of Aurelie Hebert.

Aurelie was enchanting. Her platinum-blonde hair trailed down her back in gentle waves, framing her turquoise eyes in wispy ringlets. Those eyes guaranteed our future queen never tied a shoe or carried a book as long as a teenage boy hung around. And they definitely hung around, circling Aurelie like sheep to Bo Peep.

The high school choir director compared her voice to Judy Garland. Our village gossip insisted that Carnival Cruise Lines approached Aurelie to sing on their cruises out of New Orleans. After graduation, of course.

Aurelie maintained a GPA of 4.1 while captain of the cheer-leading squad and president of the National Honor Society. During the Miss Graisseville competition, she performed Whitney Houston's *I Will Always Love You* while twirling flaming batons. Several witnesses reported tears in the judges' eyes as she captured their hearts and their votes. No other Miss Graisseville scored so high in the contest's history. Aurelie seemed destined to win the festival crown. She took her destiny seriously.

Aurelie practiced day and night for the festival, at least according to the neighbors, with Whitney's song burned into their brains. They didn't mind hearing the tune in their sleep because it was all in the name of community spirit. Aurelie's crown could put Graisseville on the map, so to speak. This win could pave the way for more tourism, leading to growth. Village growth would translate into new businesses, which would mean more jobs and, therefore, more revenue. Aurelie had the potential to transform Graisseville into a larger, more affluent community.

Six weeks before the festival, my mother-in-law Ava burst through the door of our downtown coffee shop. "Oh, it's awful, just awful! Aurelie Hebert has suffered a tragic baton accident and cannot compete at the festival. I can't believe it! What are we going to do?"

Wiping up the drops of my favorite brew as best I could, I glanced at my mother-in-law. A baton accident? How does that even happen? My best friend in high school wanted to try out for the majorette squad, so she bought a baton and began twirling. That girl practiced for hours but kept hitting herself on the head when she threw her baton in the air.

Her father finally threw her batons in the trash can. "I officially declare your twirling career finished! Our health insurance doesn't cover baton twirling injuries." Later, we discovered that wasn't true. Truthfully, though, her dad saved my friend from potential brain damage. From what I'd heard, Aurelie was much more coordinated than my friend.

Ava's voice returned me from memory lane as she wrung her hands, describing the tragedy. "Oh, it's horrible, just horrible! Aurelie was practicing with her flaming batons and singing her signature song. You know, that beautiful song by Whitney Houston! Well, the wind picked up, and a gust blew sparks off the batons into Aurelie's hair. Now, fortunately, Aurelie's father made her promise to always have a bucket of water and a hose nearby, just in case the batons caught fire to something. That quick-thinking gal ran over to the bucket and dunked her head to save the day."

My mind pictured all that long platinum hair as fuel for a fire. Thank goodness Mr. Hebert thought ahead!

"Our sweet Aurelie's quick thinking would have saved the day, except for her brother Elliott. That young man doesn't have the sense that God gave him! Why, when he was a little boy…"

Ava had a habit of going down rabbit trails before finishing her stories. I'd learned through the years that she just needed a nudge back to the main path. "Ava! What did Aurelie's brother do?"

My mother-in-law paused, frowned slightly, then found her

footing. "Oh yes! Well, Aurelie's brother was supposed to water the flowers when he got home from school. His mama had been fussing at him to get it done all afternoon. Finally, his mama yelled, *Elliott, if you don't water those flowers, I'm going to unplug that Xbox and throw it out the window!* So, Elliott got up off the couch, went outside, and poured the water into the flower bed."

By this time, all of us in the coffee shop tuned in to Ava's story. We also understood why Ava's voice had rose an octave, and her speech accelerated.

"That darn boy used Aurelie's bucket to water the flowers! And he didn't have the sense to refill it! So the poor girl didn't douse her curls with water—she just whacked her head on the bottom of the empty bucket! But Aurelie—oh, that girl's as smart as a whip! I'll give her credit for that! She ran to the faucet and turned on the hose."

Ava stopped for a breath, and we all took one with her. We'd not had this much excitement since Bob Cahill's cows got out on Highway 171, and the sheriff's deputies helped him push them off the road.

"By the time Aurelie put out her hair, most of it was gone. She ran in to get her mama, and they called Dr. Phillips. He recommended a hair and scalp specialist in Baton Rouge, and Mrs. Hebert called him next. But he said there was nothing he could do in the six weeks before the festival." Ava continued wringing her hands, as if she was wringing out a wet towel.

Our visions of a festival crown circled the drain. The Board of Aldermen called an emergency village council meeting to find a new Miss Graisseville. Ava sent her husband, so she could bake pecan sandies for Aurelie and her family. Wild horses couldn't keep me away from this meeting! How could we fix this disaster?

Mayor Ruby Bergeron spent the first fifteen minutes reviewing the facts of the situation. Aurelie had been our greatest hope, and now she could not fulfill her destiny. Three other young ladies had competed with Aurelie in the original Miss Graisseville competition. One of them fractured her wrist helping her father on the farm, and the second had gone to live with her aunt in New Orleans. The third potential Miss Graisseville temporarily resided in the parish detention center, arrested for shoplifting at the Gas n' More. She would be out on bail by the festival, but no one wanted to put that on her application. Our prospects did not look promising.

Alderman Clay Terry called for order amid the murmurs of frustration and despair.

"Ladies and gentlemen, I may have a solution. My niece, Rose Terry, has a GPA just as high as Aurelie's. She is extremely talented and blessed with her grandmother's natural Bergeron family beauty. How about we select a committee to review her qualifications and reconvene in a couple of days?" Clay looked around the room, hoping we would embrace his plan.

"That's a wonderful idea, Clay! I mean, Alderman Clay. I mean, Alderman Terry." This speech sounded better in my head. "I volunteer to be on the review committee." Not to be left out of an adventure, my best friend Maggie quickly jumped in. Looking around the room, I saw a handful of people meeting my gaze. Amy Melancon took pity on me and raised her hand to be the third member of our merry band.

Clay smiled gratefully. "Wonderful! Ava, could you nominate these fine ladies so we can vote to accept the committee. Then I suggest we meet back here in three days and hear the committee's recommendation on whether Rose Terry would be a suitable Miss Graisseville. Do I hear a second?" Clay continued as Robert's rules of order dictated, and the attendants nominated, seconded, and voted to approve our committee. The meeting adjourned, and Maggie, Amy, and I gathered around Clay.

"First, thank you for agreeing to review Rose's qualifications. I suggest you go to the high school and speak with the principal and maybe some of her teachers. You'll find she possesses an impeccable character."

The next day, we met at the coffee shop for caffeine to go. As we waited for our orders, Amy became quiet. When questioned, she hesitated a second before asking, "Have either of you seen Rose Terry?"

Maggie and I both shook our heads.

Amy continued, "The last time I saw Rose was a few weeks ago, when she came into the tractor supply store with her father. I'm not trying to be ugly—I'm really not. Rose may have natural Bergeron beauty, but she downplays it considerably with her Terry style of fashion." We encouraged Amy to continue. "The Terrys are dear, but they buy their clothes at the same store as their truck tires. Rose is just shy of six feet tall, skinny as a rail, and wears black, thick-framed glasses."

We stared back, our mouths open. Did we have time for a beauty queen makeover? Did Rose even want one? I voted to go to the high school as Clay suggested and speak with the principal. Then we could talk to Rose herself and make some decisions. A sick feeling snaked its way into my stomach, and I dumped my half-full cup of coffee into the trash.

We met with the principal, a wonderful man who gave us a rundown of Miss Rose Terry. She sounded delightful, but I was concerned about Amy's comments. "Sir, do you think Rose is a strong contestant for the festival queen competition?

That man never missed a beat. He looked me squarely in the eye. "If I was on the panel of judges for that festival, I'd vote for Rose, hands down." Oh my stars! If only he had some pull with the judges!

I phoned Rose's mother to schedule our visit. She admitted they'd attended the emergency meeting the night before but snuck out during Clay's rousing speech. She was hesitant but agreed to meet with us. As I hung up, I puzzled over Rose's reaction. Personally, I found it exciting to be part of an official village project. Who would have guessed Rose and her family didn't feel the same?

Our committee banded together outside Rose's home promptly at 7 that night, then strolled to the door and rang the bell. Rose answered, and I scrutinized her. What exactly had we gotten ourselves into?

The seventeen-year-old standing before us was sporting a black T-shirt tucked into Wrangler jeans. Her blue and black plaid long-sleeved shirt hung limply around her shoulders. Was it my imagination, or had she pulled it out of the dirty clothes and thrown it on before answering the door? Rose completed her outfit with white athletic socks and no shoes. Our backup beauty queen had pulled her dark-brown hair into a ponytail, probably before school that morning. Why did I think that? Because it was spilling out of the hairband onto her shoulders.

Amy was right! Square black oversized eyeglasses perched upon her nose, reminding me of the legendary singer/songwriter Buddy Holly. This girl might possess natural beauty, but she did her best to keep it under wraps.

Our hostess ushered us into the living room, and her parents greeted us with proper Southern hospitality. We settled into various couches and chairs while Rose's mother brought in coffee and Louisiana crunch cake. My mother-in-law, Ava, considered her own crunch cake the best in the parish. Would eating this cake be proper Southern etiquette or family betrayal? Maybe I should have a piece, so I could report my findings to Ava? I had two pieces to confirm Ava's was better. Please don't tell her, though.

Rose agreed to represent Graisseville in the festival if we could address a few concerns. First out of the gate was her choice of eyeglasses. Dr. Mercer, in nearby Zachary, could fix up Rose with some contacts. Her mother agreed to call for an appointment the next day, so we moved on to the next issue. Rose voiced the elephant in the room, her lack of fashion sense.

Hmmm...please don't look at me for advice. My idea of fashion was matching my socks to my t-shirt.

Amy piped up. "Oh, sweetie, don't you fret! Aurelie Hebert offered to give you a personal fashion consultation! You girls aren't the same height, not even close, so you can't wear her pageant clothes. But she and her mother offered to take you to Baton Rouge to fix you up with the most fashionable clothing you can afford." Even Amy lost her smile as her words sank in.

The Terrys did not value spending money on clothes, not when the tractor needed new tires. So how would we pay for Rose's pageant clothes?

Maggie came to the rescue. "Hey, ladies, I've got this! My coffee shop's not making a huge profit, but I was just talking to my husband last night, and we agreed to sponsor Rose for the festival. We can use the sponsorship money for clothes." Maggie flashed a grin at Rose. "Consider yourself clothed in pure fashion for the festival!"

Oh my goodness, God solved another problem! Last on our list: the talent competition. Uncle Clay Terry himself said this girl had loads of talent, so we were home free.

Rose's father, like most men, blurted out the obvious. "Yeah, that's fine. But Rose has no talent. What are you going to do about that?"

Thank you, Rose's father, for your positive thinking!

Fortunately, Rose had embraced the Queen of the Festival concept, so she had several ideas. "I have reviewed the rules for the festival, and there's a lot of flexibility. My talent can be dance, vocal, playing an instrument, reciting a monologue, acting, demonstrating, or something else. I think we should focus on the *something else.*"

Oh girl, do we want to know what the *something else* could be?

Rose felt we did, so she continued. "I can shear a sheep. I can milk a cow. I can whistle *You Are My Sunshine.* I can recite the poem *In the Creole Twilight*. I can call off the capitals of the United States…" She gauged our open mouths and saucer eyes.

Amy again was the voice of reason. "Rose sweetie, didn't your grandma tell me one time you enjoyed cooking?"

Rose's eyes lit up with excitement. "Yes, but I didn't think that was a festival-worthy talent. Are you saying it is?"

Amy pulled up the rules on her phone, and we gathered round, literally holding our breath. Cooking technically fell under the category of demonstration, so the committee voted to present Rose Terry and our plan to the village in two days. Rose had a fighting chance at the festival as long as she got contacts, took Aurelie Hebert's fashion advice, and cooked a fabulous dish for the judges. It seemed so simple until I laid awake that night in bed. What had I been thinking when I volunteered for the committee? Winning this festival hung on so many variables that we needed a miracle to pull this together.

We witnessed some amazing transformations as our new Miss Graisseville prepared for her festival challenges. That sweet young lady traded her sturdy glasses for contacts and took advantage of a free cut and bronze highlights from the downtown Bristle 'n' Blush. She accompanied Aurelie Hebert to Baton Rouge for a complimentary fashion consult and a pageant wardrobe courtesy of Maggie's Coffee Shop. The committee was eager to sample Rose's talent, which was her grandmother's shrimp and grits dish.

This dish is a classic recipe enjoyed all over the country, but especially south of the Mason-Dixon line. They are a staple among most Southerners, as a substitute for potatoes sand rice. Any respectable Southerner eats shrimp and grits regularly, and the Terrys were no exception.

Our community credited Rose's grandmother for creating, hands down, the most delectable shrimp and grits. She guarded her recipe like a state secret, and not even her children had access. Grandmother Terry locked all doors and shut all curtains, leaving no gaps for prying eyes. No one had any clue what took place as she whipped up her shrimp and grits. Our next miracle would be to convince Grandmother Terry to share her recipe. Her son Clay sat down with his mother and lectured her about community spirit. Grandmother Terry didn't budge. Clay brought in his brother (Rose's father) and his sister for reinforcements. The three Terry children called upon family unity, family history, and ended with describing in great detail how the family could lose this precious recipe forever if Grandmother Terry passed before sharing her secret. The woman shook her head, arms crossed tightly over her chest.

Rose took matters into her own hands. She picked up her grandmother and drove her to the cemetery to visit Grandfather Terry's grave. While gazing at her grandfather's tombstone, Rose reminisced about the time she had spent with him. She described their long walks together and how Rose sat in her grandfather's lap while he told her stories of his childhood. Grandmother Terry nodded and wiped a tear from her eye. Rose repeated stories about fishing with her grandfather, always returning with a boatload of catfish.

"You know, Grandma, I wish Grandpa Terry had given me the secret recipe for his catfish bait. Dad and I go to the same place that Grandpa did, but without his secret bait, we don't bring home nearly the number of catfish he did." She looked sideways at her grandmother to see if the woman was understanding the conversation.

Grandmother Terry sighed. "Rose, I will give you my shrimp and grits recipe. I don't want my secret to die with me like your grandfather's secret died with him. Oh, glory, that man never let anybody get near the garage when he was cooking up his secret bait! Not even his own wife!" She laughed and gave Rose a hug. "I guess I'm being selfish, but I feel like the recipe is the only thing I have that's still useful. My daughter and daughters-in-law have taken over all the cooking for every family event except the shrimp and grits. I want to feel needed, and that recipe has been the only way I've been able to do that."

Now it was Rose's turn to give her grandmother a hug. "Grandma, I cross my heart! I will not share your secret with anyone, and you can still make the shrimp and grits. I feel pretty certain that you will always make them better than me."

Grandmother Terry laughed, then said, "But I have a few conditions." That Grandmother Terry was a shrewd Southern woman. First, she made Rose swear on the family Bible in front of the entire Terry clan that she would never divulge the recipe as long as Grandmother Terry was still breathing. Rose also promised she would never make the shrimp and grits after the festival until Grandmother Terry had passed. Last, Rose promised she would be the only student in Grandmother Terry's cooking lessons, she would not share any information from those lessons, and she would not make any audio or visual recordings during that time. After making these solemn promises, Grandmother Terry granted Rose access to her kitchen. Grandmother and granddaughter spent most of the six weeks before the festival in the kitchen. Rose first had to memorize not only the recipe but also a new standard of measurement. Grandmother Terry did not use measuring cups or spoons, so Rose had to master "pinch," "smidgen," "dollop," and "dash." She also had to perfect the art of tasting. After she added each ingredient, she tasted the mixture to determine whether the proportions were correct. Rose said later she had never had so much fun in her life.

Clay contacted the festival, explained the situation, and listed Rose as our Miss Graisseville. The committee met with Rose a few days before to give her the once-over and sample her shrimp and grits. Her transformation mesmerized even the most cynical resident. I wasn't sure what Aurelie Hebert planned to do beyond high school, but she had a future as a fairy godmother. That girl seriously worked miracles, and I had already told myself to be on the lookout for some. Miracle number one had been Rose convincing her grandmother to give up her coveted shrimp and grits recipe. Miracle number two was standing before me. Rose had beautiful hazel eyes, hair the color of cinnamon, and a contagious smile. This girl had natural beauty! My sigh rested somewhere between relief and admiration. Our Cinderella was to die for!

She also made shrimp and grits that were heaven on earth. We were there to give final approval on the contestant and the dish, and we left the Terry household believing we had been in the presence of a true beauty. I told my husband Mike later that night I wanted to be buried in Rose's shrimp and grits. His mouth said *okay*, but his eyes said, *I think you're just south of crazy*. He hadn't tasted Rose's shrimp and grits, so he couldn't understand. The entire village attended the festival, including my husband and kids. Mike even closed his store, reasoning that his best customers would be at the festival. The night before, we discussed Rose's excellent chances of winning.

"Honey, what's the name of this festival?"

Mike stared at me. "You mean you don't know?"

Irritated, I snapped. "If I knew, why would I be asking?"

Mike stood in front of me, obviously to have a full view of my reaction as he responded. "Why, it's the Feathers and Fur Festival. That means if Rose wins, her title would be Queen of Feathers and Fur."

We couldn't stop laughing even as we climbed into bed. Still chuckling, I realized God had moved metaphorical mountains so my dark horse could be the Queen of Feathers and Fur.

If only I had stories to tell of the Queen of Feathers and Fur competition and the drama and suspense we endured. Of course, I'd love to say our Rose swept the title hands down. Sadly, she didn't.

Rose was a fierce competitor, but in the end, she was no match for Miss Evangeline Bordelon from Plaquemine (*Plack-Uh-Min*) Parish. Evangeline played the harmonica and the piano while singing *Dancing Queen* by ABBA. She also danced while singing and playing the harmonica, thanks to a piano on wheels and harmonica strapped to her chest. What a show-off!

The judges engorged themselves on Rose's shrimp and grits and marveled at her magic hands hiding the ingredients. Yet they still crowned Evangeline Queen of Feathers and Fur. Those obviously biased judges granted Rose First Runner-Up, so I claimed a victory on behalf of my committee. The village hosted a small yet rousing parade for Miss Rose Terry. Mayor Ruby Bergeron dug up some funds and posted a tasteful billboard just outside of the village limits. It read "Village of Graisseville: Home of First Runner-Up Queen of Feathers and Fur." A definite step toward economic growth.

THE THREAD UNCOVERED

MARGUERITE MARTIN GRAY

June 2000, Virginia

lamping her fingers around the luggage handle, Sophie Lucy Marteen soaked in the unlikely security of an inanimate object. She had no one to blame but herself. Each of her sisters had offered to go with her on this journey, but Sophie's instinct and independent streak urged her to go alone. It wasn't as if she'd never traveled abroad before. Her three months backpacking with a friend in Europe taught her the survival skills she'd carry on this trip. So why is this unexpected fear making her tighten her grip?

Her cell phone in her jeans pocket vibrated. Which sister would it be this time? Being the baby of the siblings had its benefits and nuisances. Love and concern.

"Hey, Maggie. I knew it had to be you."

Fourteen years older than Sophie's twenty-four years, Maggie had two children and played the role of Mother Maggie even now.

"Are you ready? I could still stow away in your suitcase."

Sophie smiled and sighed. "I'd better be ready since I'm walking to my boarding gate right now."

"Want to trade places?"

"Are you kidding? A vacation in England for three weeks or taking care of a nine- and ten-year-old? No offense, but I choose England."

Laughter boomed in her ear. "I know. I hope you find what you are looking for."

Me too. It's probably silly to most people, especially my sisters.

Yet, they did not have a middle name from some random non-family member. No one had the name Lucy. Her sisters had strong last names as middle names: Walker, Pleasant, and Choice. All connecting them to their ancestors. Sophie's first name went back seven generations. But Lucy? She was a strange old lady living in a manor house in Birkenhead, England. Not one drop of blood existed between them.

Sophie found her gate and an empty seat. "Give the kids my love. We'll get together in July."

One down, two more to go, plus her parents. Then Sophie planned to put her phone away for a few days. She had all the information she needed in a notebook.

Lady Lucy Landon.

What was her mother thinking? Sophie's question didn't hinge on disappointment. More like curiosity and confusion. *I'm named after a friend of the family who lives in England. Will she even want to see me? At least I know she's alive and living at the same address, although her husband passed away a few years ago.*

Giggling brought a few glances her way. Her imagination zoomed ahead to a doorstep. "Hello, I'm from Virginia in the United States. I want to be properly introduced to the lady who shares my name. Or I share your name. However, it goes."

After that, the rest of the trip was Sophie's to do whatever she wanted. She had reservations in the Cotswolds and on down to Cornwall. First things first. The tracing of the Lucy connection.

1972 Birkenhead, England

Lucy Landon surveyed the dark-paneled salon at the back of her rambling manor house. Much too dark and dreary. Old. But her husband Mark loved it. He said it oozed history and family. Well, yes. Three hundred years of the past spread through the forty-plus rooms. The manor begged for children, but they had none. Lord and Lady Landon had it all—titles, money, land—all the trappings that one might say mattered—with no one to share it.

Rolling an antique tea cart, her housekeeper and companion, Claire, maneuvered her way around the old and new furniture to a spot free of clutter.

"Thank you, Claire. When my guests arrive, please bring them in here. I think the little girls will be more comfortable in the less formal room." *The truth? I'm more comfortable in my oversized stuffed twentieth-century chair and ottoman than in the antique straight-backed ones in every room.* The ornate settees weren't any better. But one must keep up appearances—lineage and all that rubbish. At least her guests had no need for connections and probably didn't care about the peerage.

Americans. A sweet family she'd met at St. Saviour's Church. Their daughters—ten, eight, and six years old—contained their energy for the most part while they were still allowed to be curious little girls. American? British? French? Girls would be girls. Just what this house needed for an afternoon.

Mark's whistle preceded his entrance. She grinned at her still handsome husband. Forty years of marriage. *We've both aged well. Not bad for sixty and sixty-five.* His tweed jacket had made it through the ages. White hair and glasses befitted the lord of the manor. He'd do for the Americans.

Patting her shoulder-length silver hair in place, Lucy wondered if her navy skirt and white blouse with only a few ruffles would blend well with the casual afternoon tea. She could ditch her heels for more comfortable shoes but decided her role as lady of the house demanded a bit of polish.

Mark fiddled with his pipe before returning it to his pocket. He must have remembered "no smoking around the girls." Claiming his post in a big leather chair, Mark crossed his heel over his knee. "I'm rather excited about talking to Mr. Marteen about architecture. He's all into the preservation stuff. Wonder what he'll think of this monstrosity stuck on the outskirts of the village?"

Hardly a village. "I'm glad you've found a common ground since I'm no good at that subject. I'm more interested in Ann and the girls. How brave to bring the whole family to England. I don't think I could have done that." Perhaps given the chance, she would have done adventurous things with her children. If...

Lucy turned to the salon door at the first sound of voices. "They're here."

He winked at her. "It's going to be fine. You've entertained thousands of times—dukes and dignitaries."

"I know, but not little girls."

The trio of girls bounded into the room, wide-eyed and silent. At least, they'd all met before at church. Ann and George followed, not as awed as the children, more studious and curious. Lucy set her shoulders and assumed the hostess persona. "Welcome, come in. We'll have tea in here. I hope you didn't have any trouble finding us."

Ann directed the girls to a long couch. "Not at all. Thank you, Lucy, for the invitation. Everyone has been so welcoming in the parish."

She settled the girls before straightening her pleated hunter-green skirt. "This is a treat. I promise the girls will be well-behaved. We've already been in many National Trust houses with 'no touch' rules."

Lucy laughed, breaking loose from her rigid lady manners. "Ah, Ann, this is a home, yearning for a few mishaps, bumps, and scrapes." She surveyed the walls and shelves with antique knick-knacks. "A few broken pieces in exchange for giggles and games will do our souls some good."

George found Mark, and already they were deep in conversation about architecture or history—something other than politics and billiards. Lucy couldn't imagine the jolly American smoking a cigar with a glass of port in a tuxedo. George Marteen, in his brown pants and casual sports jacket, exuded confidence without the snobby British trimmings.

Lucy wanted this friendship, a chance to experiment with a laid-back attitude. "Let's fill our plates and relax a bit. Then, the girls can play in the garden while we get to know each other." She glanced at the grinning girls. "But first, tell me your names again."

The stairsteps answered. "Maggie." "Sarah." "Christine." Beautiful girls with bright smiles, freckled cheeks, and sparkling blue eyes, ready for the next adventure.

Turning to the tea cart, Lucy scrutinized the selection, hoping her menu suited the girls. "I have an assortment of sandwiches. The cucumber and pâté ones might not be to your liking, but I have cheese and ham too. Shortbread, raspberry tarts, cream puffs, cheese straws, ginger biscuits. Well, you can try them all. Let the girls go first. I set up a table for them."

In the role of hostess, Lucy could do well. But a friend was a different matter. Perhaps, this one would last. Forget the years.

Half an hour later, the girls ran through the manicured hedges and paths and played chase and hide-and-seek. The gardens never shone as bright and healthy.

Thank you, Lord, for these girls. Make my heart open to new friend-ships. Use this home and us to benefit others.

Open our doors? Yes, to the Americans, and why not our own neighbors?

2000, Birkenhead

Sophie had no recollection of her time spent in Birkenhead in the summer of 1980. She was not even four years old. All she knew came from stories her parents and sisters told. Was she crazy trying to do this? Her mother thought it a brilliant idea. Maybe. But what would the octogenarian think of Sophie's plan?

Getting behind the wheel of her rental car after her train arrived in the city, though not a new experience, did take mental and kinetic adjustments. Her right and left fought for dominance. At least her Airbnb took minutes and not hours to find.

The guest house faced a lovely city park with paths, trees, and flowers. Someone cared about the vegetation. After unpacking her small suitcase, Sophie put the Landon estate address in her GPS. Only one and a half miles. Why not tackle her anxiety about meeting a stranger unannounced with an afternoon stroll?

Sophie checked her hair, applied a little face powder, and changed her travel clothes for a fresh yellow blouse and blue capri pants. A quick glance in a full-length mirror spurred her into action. Presentable.

It's not as if I'm going to meet the queen.

No, just Lady Lucy Landon. Just the name intimidated her. No one she'd ever met that she remembered added Lady to a name.

Maybe I should change. Do I look too plain? Too American? She giggled. *I am American. Not an ounce of ladyship in me. I've dreamed of this for a few years. Smile, Miss Sophie Lucy Marteen. She'll love me.*

Almost forgetting the gifts from her mother, Sophie rummaged to find the package. If nothing else, Sophie could say, "I come bearing gifts from afar."

Energized by her quest, Sophie, strolling through the neighborhoods, snapped photos of the colorful doors and quaint cottages with small English gardens. Her mom adopted the style of gardening by using a variety of seeds and bulbs in no particular design, lending an artist's touch to the flower beds.

As one mile melted away, the houses and landscapes changed. Cottages and duplexes became small manor houses until she halted in front of an enormous old brick mansion looming behind a brick wall enclosing the grounds. Her GPS indicated this as the place, but Sophie's mind shouted, "Wouldn't I have remembered this?"

The wrought iron gate opened onto a gravel path with manicured lawns on each side. The three-story structure with white framed window panes, though ancient—perhaps seventeenth century, according to her parents—welcomed more than intimidated Sophie. Were servants relegated to the third floor as in all the novels she'd read and seen played out in the houses she'd visited in England on her backpacking tour? Or did Lady Landon live alone in the monstrous house?

Sophie decided to use her teaching skills she practiced daily with her music students to calm herself. One eighty-eight-year-old lady couldn't be as nerve-racking as twenty high schoolers.

She knocked twice and stepped back, lacing her hands around the package.

The door opened, and a middle-aged woman in a peach-colored blouse and a knee-length, black skirt greeted Sophie with a smile. "Good afternoon. How may I help you?"

Once she opened her mouth, the woman would know she was not a local. That fact buoyed her, proud to be from across the pond. "Hello. I'm Sophie Marteen. Is Lady Landon at home? I have a gift for her from my parents."

The woman's grin reached her eyes as her hands extended toward Sophie as if to hug her, stopping just short, resting her hands instead on Sophie's upper arms. "I know who you are, Miss Lucy. I recognize you now from your family's Christmas card. I'm Mary Atkins. Lady Lucy will be so happy to see you. Come in, please."

Mrs. Atkins' enthusiasm engulfed Sophie, making her want to complete the hug. The expansive entrance faced a grand staircase and multiple doors on each side of the foyer. The wood shone as if recently polished. The chandelier's crystals sent spiraling rainbow patterns across the tiled floor.

They veered to the right toward large open double doors. "Wait here. I need to give Lady Lucy a little warning. I won't tell her your name, though."

Sophie beamed with confidence. *God sent me here. This is His plan. So, it's Okay.*

"Come in." Mrs. Atkins nodded, her now permanent grin even wider.

Stepping into a bright, white-walled room, in contrast to the dark foyer, Sophie searched for her namesake. An elegant, tall, white-haired woman stood by the fireplace, staring at Sophie. In slow motion, Lady Landon raised her hands to her mouth, then opened her arms.

"Sophie Lucy Marteen, welcome home."

1980, Birkenhead

"Mark, they're here. Oh, I can't believe it."

She's here. Four years old already. Lucy looked up and down, peeking through the front curtains of the drawing room.

So many questions. *Would the Marteen girls remember me? Would*

Anne and I pick up where we left off? Would my namesake want anything to do with an older version of Lady Landon?

I am old. Or at least older. Sixty-eight must be ancient to teenage girls.

Lucy ran her hands down her lavender skirt that billowed at the bottom and swirled as she walked. Something summery to lighten up the dark paneled rooms. The one thing she didn't like about living in an old house meant for preservation was the inability to change the color of the walls. To keep it authentic to the seventeenth century, the dark stains and paneling had to stay. At least Mark allowed her to place bright, cheery rugs in some of the rooms.

Stop. This is not about the carpet, the walls, or my skirt. This time it's about my American friends and Sophie Lucy—a four-year-old carrying my name.

When Ann had written and asked permission to name the child, Lucy had sunk into her chair. Ann desired to name her fourth daughter after her. More than yes, Lucy felt honored and privileged. With no children or grandchildren, Lucy recognized this thread of life as significant. Somewhere in the world, her legacy—her name—would continue. It certainly didn't matter that the child had no blood ties. Not even British. No. What mattered was the potential for connection, for love.

Mark stood tall and confident in the foyer with his hands holding the lapels of his old tweed jacket. Hopefully, not the same one he wore eight years ago. Oh, well. They could afford a whole new wardrobe, but why bother?

He rolled back on his heels. "He, ho, my dear. Isn't this exciting? Remembering us after all these years."

"Only eight years, yet so much has happened."

Lucy dabbed her eyes. A baby. A little Lucy. Surely, Ann and George didn't regret the name choice. Of course not. Sophie Lucy might but not her parents. It was purposeful. Prayerful.

Lucy and Mark shooed the butler and housekeeper away and opened the front door wide before anyone could knock.

Six Marteens—not five—greeted them. Lucy's eyes teared. "Oh, my. Let me look at you all. Just lovely." The three older girls didn't stairstep anymore. The teenagers wore jeans and T-shirts and had long hair, large smiles, and perfect teeth. Eighteen, sixteen, and fourteen.

After hugs from Ann, George, and the older girls, Lucy swept them inside to a formal sitting room. Mark cornered George and began the list of questions about mutual interests. They'd be busy for a while.

Lucy motioned to the chairs and couches. She needed to sit even if they didn't. "Please sit down for a few minutes before lunch in the dining room."

Ann sat and put the youngest in her lap. "I hope you didn't go to too much trouble. We just had to see you. I want you to meet Sophie Lucy. This is Lady Lucy Landon. You share the same name."

The curly-haired blonde with large blue eyes tilted her head and reached for Lucy. "I know you. You are the pretty lady in a Christmas card." She scooted off her mother's lap and stood in front of Lucy. "I'm glad we have the same name. I don't know anyone else who has it." Aiming her small arms upward, Sophie Lucy hugged her namesake's neck and kissed her cheek.

Tears pricked in Lucy's eyes at the innocent, loving gesture. Lucy held her tight for a second. "I'm glad to meet you. I knew I would like anyone who shared my name."

Sophie Lucy leaned closer and whispered. "Can I call you Lady Lucy? It's a lot prettier than your other name. You know, the long one. And you can call me Lucy."

"I like that plan. Lucy and Lady Lucy. I heard you like something called macaroni and cheese? And fish cut up into little sticks?"

Little Lucy smacked her lips. "I sure do. They didn't have any on the plane. Do you have some here?"

"I do. Specially ordered for you."

The child found her sisters and tried to sit still.

Lucy studied the girls. "We'll go outside in the garden after lunch. Maggie, do you remember when you were here before?"

"Oh, yes, ma'am. We all do. We'll teach Sophie our games."

Lady Lucy pulled a heavy rope, hanging from the ceiling by the mantle, ringing for service. This would be the best meal she'd had in a long time.

Friendships across the miles and time. A new lifelong thread with a precious child.

Birkenhead, 2000

Home? Sophie expected any other welcome than that. Home was for a family with deep roots, not for a wandering American who showed up unannounced on the doorstep. But home? Sophie closed her eyes for half a second and opened them to find Lady Lucy's open arms.

What do I do? Fall into them? Back away? Stand still? Her own arms took control as she stepped into the hug—melted was a better word.

Why did people stereotype the British as cold and standoffish? Lady Lucy wasn't that way at all, at least not today with Sophie.

Dropping her arm across Sophie's shoulders, the tall, older woman led her into a bright space by the window with an expansive view of the front lawn. A tea table rested there with four comfy chairs for reading, corresponding, or talking for hours. Sophie expected to see a cat curled up in a chair next to the bookcase.

"Mrs. Atkins is preparing a few items for tea. Will you stay?"

Stay? Of course. For how long? Sophie giggled. Forever? "I'd love to visit for a while. I hope you don't mind the intrusion." Sophie chose an overstuffed chair with a pink rose pattern. She had a perfect view of Lady Lucy and the rose garden.

Sophie's stare matched her hostess' blue gaze. Her hands started talking as if she were in her classroom. If only she could claim the floor as a stage. "I know my showing up unexpected is strange. My whole trip is an impulse. I was so young when I was here before. I need to know. Why you? Why your name?" Sophie's hand covered her heart. "Is my name more than a whim from my mom?"

Through glistening tears, Lady Lucy reached for Sophie's wayward hands and held them in hers. "Ever since Ann asked me if she could name you Lucy, I have felt an overwhelming connection with you. It is strange, but people do it all the time. They name their child after a movie star or a sports figure or a king or president. History is full of examples. But for me, Sophie Lucy, I felt a thread binding us. It's more than a name."

Sophie watched her. "And this thread, what does it mean?"

"That part is easy. Love. This thread is love."

Tilting her head at the revelation, Sophie laughed, a pure deep sound of joy. "Love. That is the best answer you could have given me."

After their round of laughter, they sealed their link with a cup of tea, delicate cucumber sandwiches, and a scone with raspberry jam and clotted cream.

Lady Lucy balanced her tea cup and saucer as only an English woman could. "I don't suppose you'd consider changing your plans and staying here for a while?"

Oh, wouldn't I? "If that's an invitation, I'll be here tomorrow."

"Wonderful. My great-nephew arrives this weekend. He's about your age, and I have a feeling you'll get along splendidly."

If Lady Lucy could devise plans, so could Sophie. "I don't suppose you'd want to join me in Cornwall for a few weeks?"

"You'd travel with an old lady on your holiday?"

"No. But I'd travel with you. Let's make up for missed opportunities."

"No, not missed opportunities. The thread had to pull you here for you to understand."

The future swung wide open with possibilities. The name was only one thread, only the beginning of their love and friendship.

HERITAGE OF HOPE

CAROLE LEHR JOHNSON

Cornwall, England
Spring 1645

The inky night sky shone brightly with sparkling stars reflected in the rippling tide. Melior Olford tugged her wool shawl tighter around her shoulders.

"Nay, Will." She shoved the young man away.

"Mellie, I but desire a departing kiss from my betrothed." He whispered a soft endearment into her ear. "My love."

She closed her eyes and leaned back against the rough stone outcropping, gentle waves lapping close to their hidden spot at the edge of the beach below the cliffs.

The screech of a tawny owl sounded overhead, and Melior gasped at the sudden noise. "I must go, or else I shall be missed."

He wrapped his arms around her slender frame, his voice lowered, breath shaking. "I shall miss you."

"And I you." Her fingertips lingered as she moved a strand of dark hair from his brow. "Please come home."

"I go to fight for all that is good. How shall I not come home?"

He swept his lips across hers with tender care. When she responded, the kiss grew desperate. A dark belief murmured in her ear they would never meet again.

"Where have ye been, girl?" The force in Lord Olford's stormy eyes held her still.

Melior's palms dampened, and she shivered. "Papa, I but went for a brief walk. The night is pleasant, and the air does smell sweet." She kept her gaze from his, focusing outside the window and on the stars hovering over the calm sea.

Did Will remain at the entrance to the cave awaiting her signal? Why should he? On the morrow, he would be away to become a soldier to fight in the Royalist army. The intense thought returned —would she see him again?

Tears threatened as her father's anger rose to new heights. During the entire display, her mother sat in her customary chair, knuckles white on the dark wooden arms, firelight revealing her pale face.

The wind appeared to fully release from Lord Olford. He collapsed into the chair opposite his wife and buried his face in his hands. "Away to bed, Melior. I nay longer want to look upon your face until the morrow."

Without a word, Melior fled to her bedchamber. Her maid had laid a fire, and two candles burned in the room. She took one and placed it on the deep windowsill, swinging the shutters outward, the signal light letting Will know she was safely home.

The salt-scented air flowed into the room, and she poked her head into the breeze, squinting to see if she could catch a last glimpse of her love. After a few moments of scanning the place where they parted, Melior saw a shifting shadow pass across the moonlit sand. He was away into battle—only God knew the outcome.

The maid brushed Melior's long brown hair and regarded her in the mirror, her gaze somber.

"Eulalia, why the sad countenance?"

She pursed her lips. "Since we be friends, I shall speak plain, Mellie. I have a few years on ye and have seen much." Hesitantly, she continued. "I do know what goes on between ye and Master William."

Melior jerked her chin up and gave the woman a hard stare, eyes misting. "I know not of what ye speak."

Eulalia shook her head slowly. "Oh, my dear. Fear not that I would share this. I want not for ye to regret . . ."

"Regret what?" Melior wrung her hands in her lap. "Please speak what is on your heart."

With one last stroke of the brush, Eulalia began pinning Melior's hair into a stylish twist. "Master William has left this morn to fight for our king." Her voice shook. "I fear he shall not return and want not your heart broken."

The women stared at one another's reflection. Eulalia knelt beside Melior and wrapped her into a motherly hug, their tears flowing.

"I know of your love and wish it could be so, yet ye know the Ellery family has grand hopes for Master William, even though he be the younger son. Though your father bears a title, they still would not wish him to marry the daughter of a near-impoverished family. 'Tis not in the Ellery's plans."

Melior's sobs that had ebbed and flowed like the sea for many days were finally released. Will had been gone for weeks, yet she had naught but one missive from him, his promise to often write not being fulfilled. The letter had come a fortnight after his departure, proclaiming his love for her and detailing plans for their future.

"Eulalia," she choked on her tears. "I miss him. I love him."

Eulalia patted Melior's back, her own tears dotting the bodice of her gray dress. "I know, my dear. The waiting be the hardest. Yet God has a plan, and His good shall be done whatever happens."

Melior, more pale-faced and thin than the day William Ellery went to war, felt the harsh wind blowing atop the cliffs overlooking Trerose Harbor. As she trudged the path, gulls cried overhead, eyeing the surf for a meal.

Each day that passed, her tears lessened, but the crack in her heart grew wider and deeper. The rough-hewn bench at the bend in the path lay ahead, and when she reached it, she pushed aside the pink thrift and collapsed onto the seat, allowing her small basket to rest at her feet. Cook had read the growing pain in her eyes, and Melior knew the kindly woman only wanted to distract her by asking if she would go to Mrs. Pittard's in Trerose for damson tarts.

Eager for an excuse to leave the manor, she gladly set out on the errand, believing the fresh air and sun may revive her. While she tried to relax, focusing on the music of the skylark's song, butterflies fluttering about, and the soothing rhythm of the waves, her mind drifted to the quiet, sweet hours spent with . . . She could not say nor think his name without melting into a puddle of tears. A sonnet of Shakespeare's came to her—one that he had quoted, which mentioned the song of the lark at daybreak.

Haply I think on thee, and then my state,
Like to the lark at break of day arising . . .

She was so weary of it all. With angry force, she jerked a handkerchief from her bodice and wiped her eyes. Bolting to her feet, she staggered and spoke with strength she did not feel.

"I shall go on. He shall return to me!"

Melior snatched the basket into a firm grip and took long strides toward the village.

Rounding the corner onto Fore Street, she stumbled into a man who gripped her upper arms in a firm, steadying hold.

"Mistress, are ye well?" His brown eyes looked over her shoulder as if someone made to do her harm.

Radigan Atwood stood not much taller than she. He was a muscular man with thick, wavy, dark hair and had always shown her kindness and respect. At times she felt he did so with a glimmer of desire in his intense gaze. The man was but a few years her elder and had never wed.

The feel of his hands on her arms brought memories of Will's touch, and the flood of tears resurfaced. She trembled and mentally shook them away.

"Mistress Melior, ye are cold. I think ye be unwell. Come. I shall take ye into The Sands for warm ale."

She opened her mouth to refuse, but he guided her a few steps along the lane to The Burning Sands, Trerose's only tavern. His family owned the establishment, and he would eventually take charge when his father could nay longer manage.

Before she could gather the courage to turn away, she was inside the tavern, wide dark beams overhead, candles and lanterns dotted throughout. He led her to a crudely made table and eased her onto a bench.

"Sit here, and I shall fetch ye something to warm your insides." He studied her for a long moment, a scowl growing. "Ye do look a mite thinner of late. A bowl of stewed beef shall fatten ye up a bit." His smile transformed his face into a most handsome and charming visage, and her heart thawed a little.

All strength abandoned her the way Will had. What was she

now feeling? She had lost all sense of time. How long had he been gone? Five, six weeks? She cupped her cold cheeks. Nay, it was gone on two months now.

Mr. Atwood, still standing over her, said, "Ye *are* unwell, Mistress Melior. Please calm yourself, and I shall return with ale and vittles."

She nodded for lack of speech as the serving maids, men's voices, raucous laughter, and the clatter of dishes drummed around the considerable room.

As promised, Mr. Atwood returned with a steaming bowl of stewed beef and a mug of warm ale. He perched across from her. "Please eat. Ye look to be as thin as a rake these days." His concerned tone and the warmth of his eyes lulled Melior into a trance. She spooned a small bite of the meat into her mouth. The tasty morsel soothed her battered spirit, and she continued eating, surprised at her hunger. Mr. Atwood spoke of daily, mundane matters, watching her eat.

As she sipped the ale, an occasional familiar word would capture her attention, and she would smile or nod. Each time she did so, his handsome grin would reveal bracketing lines around his mouth—a very fetching mouth, she admitted. He was a pleasant man to look upon in a rugged, sea-faring way. The thought puzzled her as she knew him not to be of the sea.

A door slammed with force, bounding against the wall. Their heads snapped up, and they watched a stout, elderly woman hurrying toward them. Mr. Atwood stood, his gaze swinging to Melior's.

"I shall return shortly. Dora, our cook, has a short fuse."

Melior saw him place an arm around the woman, muttering. The only words she caught were 'new kitchen maid.'

Noting the hour must be late, she rose, retrieved her basket, and waited to thank him for his kindness.

Mr. Atwood strode toward her with a slight frown. "Are ye certain ye are able to walk the journey home?"

"I am. I must go to Mrs. Pittard's and buy tarts for our cook. Then I am away home. I thank ye for your kindness. I had a—quite pleasant time, Mr. Atwood."

She curtsied and took a step toward the door, and he stepped in front of her and held the door open. "Ye are most welcome, Mistress Melior." He dipped his head almost shyly. "Ye may do me a favor in return."

Melior swallowed hard. "If 'tis in my power to do so."

His becoming smile returned. "I should be pleased if ye would call me Radigan."

The balmy August evening met Melior as she walked toward the village, anger still roiling at Will's insistence on joining forces with the Royalist army. Each time she felt betrayed, his voice echoed in her mind. 'I go for ye, Mellie. God has called me to battle. Would ye have me tell Him nay?'

She halted under the canopy of trees and spoke aloud. "Will, I would have ye to stay here." Her tears had ceased weeks ago when she had bumped into Radigan near the tavern, broken and weary. The warm compassion he had shown her touched the shattered part of her heart where Will had lived. In the weeks following, she had seen Radigan many times. It seemed he appeared wherever she went and always surprised her with some small trinket—a flower, colorful shells from the sea, or a tasty sweet, his eyes glinting with affection.

The day news came of Will, Radigan was the bearer. How he discovered of their relationship, she knew not, yet it did not appear to trouble him.

He found her sitting on the bench overlooking the harbor, a

small book of prayer on her lap. She turned her gaze to him and smiled. "Good morrow to ye, Radigan."

He wore a grim expression as he sat next to her. "Melior, it is with sorrow I must bear this news. A man came to The Sands and did tell of . . ." He paused, seeming to collect the hard words. ". . . your *friend*, Master William—" He exhaled a long breath.

Stunned, Melior peered deep into his pained eyes.

Radigan wiped his palms down the length of his thighs and cupped his knees. "Master William died at Naseby."

With concerted effort, she looked across the sea toward where her love had perished. She closed her eyes and whispered, "I knew you would never return."

Tears came not, only dry sobs of cavern-deep grief. Strong arms wrapped around her quaking body, and she drew strength from Radigan's presence.

The low rumble of his voice in her hair soothed the broken shell she had become. "Melior, I shall care for ye if ye but allow it."

Footsteps crunched on the pebbled path and brought her gaze around to meet Will's elder brother, Gerence Ellery. The agony in his eyes mirrored her own. They held one another's regard for a time. He nodded curtly and walked away, hands clasped behind his back, knuckles white.

Acting as if he had not seen Mr. Ellery, Radigan continued, "Wed me, Melior. I have loved ye since ye were but a girl."

Startled by the revelation, she stood, not meeting his eyes. "Allow me time, Radigan. Ye have been a good and true friend, and I wish not to hurt ye."

He rose and rested gentle hands on her shoulders. "'Tis as it should be. Think on it. I shall give ye a good living, mayhap not in a manor, but a goodly life." Radigan dipped his chin and left her pondering the future—one without her true love.

Eulalia stood over Melior's bed with fists on her hips. "Mellie, ye cannot lie abed each day. Your father shall call Doctor Pooke, and eager he shall be to bleed ye." The maid shuddered with disgust.

Melior turned toward the window and saw the sun well up, brightening her chamber in a golden glow. The thought of the doctor with his jar of leeches and sharp metal objects to bleed the lifeblood from her brought images of Will lying on a muddy battlefield, red mingling with the wet earth. Her eyes burned, and her head told her it was time to move forward, but her heart screamed nay.

With sluggish movements, she sat at the edge of the bed, Eulalia still in a fighting stance. She caught her reflection in the mirror of her dressing table. Red-rimmed eyes mocked her amid a puffy face, her visage beyond startling.

Without looking at her maid, she said, "Eulalia, please help me."

"'Tis about time." She took Melior's arm to assist her.

Melior flapped her hand in dismissal. "Ye misunderstand."

Eulalia straightened. "How so?"

"Help me learn to live again. I care not should I live nor die." She raked shaking fingers through tangled hair.

"Ye are grieving. 'Tis expected. Do not give in to the grief."

Melior dropped her head into trembling hands. "I know not how to do what ye ask. 'Tis hard to place one foot before the other." She lifted her head to her maid's scrutiny.

Eulalia shot her a bemused look. "Mayhap ye should see that new young Doctor Keast near Talland Sands. I hear tell he be a good soul and takes nay stock in bleeding, leeches, and such."

Melior considered the advice for a moment, dismissing it as her parents would not allow her to do so. After persuading her into a warm bath, Eulalia dressed Melior for what the day held.

Gazing through the thick glass, Melior watched boats come and go in Trerose Harbor. Eulalia tidied her chamber, chatting about taking a walk in the gardens or going to the stable to see the new kittens.

With tepid nonchalance, Melior said, "Eulalia, Radigan Atwood asked me to wed him." The maid took in a sharp breath but said naught. "Do ye have nay words?"

The maid humphed. "Only to ask if ye accepted."

"He agreed that I should think on it."

"And have ye?" Eulalia came to stand beside her, reading her face with care.

"Nay." Melior strode to the tea tray a maid had delivered only moments before and poured a cup of tea, steam lifting. She sipped, closing her eyes, savoring the flow of hot liquid. "Should I accept?"

"Ye do not love him."

"'Tis truth. Yet I have become fond of him. He is most respectful and says he has loved me a long while."

"Aye. I have seen how he looks at ye."

"Do ye believe I could learn to love again?" Melior tapped the edge of the cup absentmindedly, and cleared her throat. "Over time?"

Melior knew there was nay disrespect intended when her maid sat at the table with her. They had become the closest of friends in the years they had been together. She poured Eulalia a cup of tea. They sat in comfortable silence for some time before Eulalia asked, "What does your heart tell ye?"

She hung her head. "I know not. Yet I know I may nay longer live here, and there is nay place for me to go."

The maid's eyes narrowed. "Why must ye leave?"

"My parents objected to Will, as ye know. They now want to force me into an arranged marriage." She clenched her teeth and stared at Eulalia.

"I know not what to do, Mellie, but ye must pray first. God will guide ye."

Melior struggled until she could stand the indecision nay longer. She must do *something*. The day fast approached until her parents' choice of a husband was to arrive at the manor for an introduction.

"Eulalia," Melior whispered, "do not forget to pack my new cloak."

"Mellie, are ye sure ye should not speak with your parents again afore ye run away?"

"Nay. The time is now. Rad is waiting."

Fast-paced footsteps sounded in the hall, and her door flew open, crashing into the wall. Her father caught it on the rebound in his meaty hand. "What is this I hear?" His gaze swung to Eulalia. "Ye—ye have aided her in this abominable liaison!"

Melior flung herself in her father's path. "Nay, she knows nothing. Blame her not."

"If ye want that raffish *tavern* worker, go to him. Radigan Atwood may have ye." He pivoted to leave, then swung back, red-faced, and pointed to Eulalia. "Take your maid with ye. I shall not have a traitor in my house." He banged the door shut, sending shivers up Melior's spine.

The small chapel at the center of Trerose lay shrouded in heavy mist. Melior gripped the bouquet of wildflowers in sweaty palms, Eulalia at her side.

"Ye do not have to go through with this, Mellie," Eulalia murmured.

"I must. *We* must. Rad has given ye a job at The Sands. All shall be well." She squeezed her friend's hand and forced a timid smile.

"We shall live above the tavern until Rad finds a cottage. Ye said ye like the small dwelling he found for ye, and 'tis near the tavern."

"Aye. 'Tis." Eulalia studied her. "What are ye not telling me, Mellie?"

Melior avoided her gaze. "'Tis naught." She leaned in and whispered, "Only Will could have made me happy. I wed now to survive. Rad is a good man. There may not be another chance to find one who is kind and caring."

Melior's ears perked as a mistle thrush sang its wild, haunting song in a nearby tree. The sapphire sky was now clear, wispy clouds floating lazily. Could the tiny creature sense a storm coming? The small birds always sang happily through a tempest. She brushed off the gloomy thought, prayed for a peaceful future, and felt a surge of hope. A scripture from her cousin, Vicar Olford, replaying in her mind.

Behold the fowls of the air: for they sow not, neither do they reap, nor gather into barns; yet your heavenly Father feedeth them. Are ye not much better than they?

Melior's emotions calmed, and she looked forward to her new life as Radigan Atwood's wife, living a heritage of hope.

THE END

Author's Note

Melior Olford is a character in my 2022 release, *The Burning Sands*. This short story reveals how Melior came to be married to Radigan Atwood. To discover how their story ends, check out *The Burning Sands* for sale wherever books are sold, in paperback and e-book.

KATHERINE'S TABLE

BEVERLY FLANDERS

*H*er arms were weighed down with plastic grocery bags as she fumbled to fit her key into the lock. She gave the door an extra hip bump to make it open, barely making it to the kitchen island to set down her unbalanced load. Her thoughts rambled as she restocked her pantry shelves. It was the same story played again and again since Katie began her widow's journey two years ago.

I just spent a small fortune at the grocery store, so why can't I think of anything to fix for supper? Planning and cooking meals for only one is a nuisance.

The blinking red light on her answering machine caught her attention. She pressed the "Play" button.

"Katie, this is your cousin, Laura Katherine. I'm in the process of downsizing so I can move into a small apartment. Are you busy this weekend? I have some family stuff I want to bring you. We can catch up on our visiting while we're at it. I'll call back later."

Katie was glad to hear from her cousin. They were close growing up and had some great times together at their grandparents' farm every summer. Laura Katherine was older, but they didn't notice the seven-year age difference between them when there was a hayloft to play in and fresh vegetables to pick. They only lived 100 miles apart now, but it might as well be 1,000. Their lives had gone separate ways as they raised their children, but they saw each other at the annual family reunions. She wondered what family memorabilia her cousin was talking about.

Katie looked around the bright yellow kitchen, and her mind swirled as she made plans for the weekend. Her housekeeping chores needed more attention than she had given them lately, so she felt the urgency to get busy.

Laura Katherine called back that evening to make definite plans. For two days, Katie cleaned her house, bought new sheets for the guest room bed, arranged fresh flowers from her garden, dusted knickknacks more thoroughly than usual, and made her small cottage-style home sparkle again.

On Saturday, Katie was ready. Fresh coffee brewed in the kitchen as she sat in her comfy green recliner in the living room. To pass the time, she thumbed through the latest issue of Southern Living Magazine. She glanced out the large bay window occasionally in anticipation of Laura Katherine's arrival.

She heard the car coming before she saw it in her driveway. She ran to the car, and the cousins greeted each other with big hugs and immediately began catching up on family news.

"Look what I brought!" Laura Katherine pointed to a small, antique, marble-topped oak table resting on the back seat of her car.

"It's the *Katherine* table!" Katie clapped her hands in delight.

"It's yours now. Unfortunately, I don't have room for it in my new place, so you're next in line to inherit it."

Through the years, the family had a tradition of passing this beautiful heirloom down to the next one in the family with *Katherine* in her name. The tradition started with Katie's and Laura Katherine's grandmother, Katherine Marie. She passed it down to her daughter, Charlotte Katherine, and she passed it on to her daughter, Laura Katherine. Now it belonged to her, Katherine Anne (also known as Katie), the daughter of Katherine Marie's son, Bill. This antique table held special memories for all of them.

Katie recalled that it sat in front of the living room window at Gram's house. She loved the marble top that sat on the spindled legs. Her grandmother used it as a display surface for assorted family pictures. There was a center drawer that always held a renewable supply of peppermints that Gram kept stashed away for visiting grandchildren to find.

"It's a little worse for wear and showing signs of age," Laura Katherine replied, apologizing for its condition. Katie looked at it lovingly and identified with its wobbly legs.

"The scratches aren't too bad. I think a good furniture restorer can fix those." Laura Katherine's suggestion was accurate, and Katie silently wished for a restorer to fix her own flaws and wobbles.

"I have the perfect place for it," Katie announced as they carried their treasure inside.

Laura Katherine smiled as she remembered her childhood days. "Mama and I
always displayed framed photographs on the marble top, just like Gram did."

The cousins carried their prize into Katie's living room and gently placed it under her window.

"My new table looks like it was made for that spot," Katie gushed. Laura Katherine and Katie stepped back to admire it and agreed, in unison, with its perfect placement.

Laura Katherine sat on Katie's overstuffed sofa. "That table was heavier than I expected. Let's rest a minute and enjoy its beauty." She nestled into the plush cushions, obviously more interested in rest than the table's beauty.

"I hate to admit it, but I used the middle drawer as my junk drawer. I emptied it before I brought it. I think I got everything out, but I should have put some peppermints in it for old times' sake." Laura Katherine smiled at the cheerful memory. In honor of their grandmother, Katie made a mental note to keep a few peppermints in the middle drawer.

Katie couldn't conceal her excitement as she walked over to the table and touched the drawer with the crystal knob. As she gave it a slight tug and reached into the empty space, a splinter scratched the top of her hand. She tried to break off the wooden sliver, but it was attached to a panel that dropped into the empty drawer space.

"Look at this!" Katie exclaimed. "A letter, a newspaper clipping, and a picture were hidden in that cubbyhole. Did you know that compartment was there?"

"I've never seen it before. I don't think Mama knew it was there either—she never showed it to me or mentioned it. All I know is that Gram was very protective of the table and insisted that it must stay in the family. I often wondered why it had so much sentimental value to her." The women added curiosity to their excitement.

"Let's see if the things we just found give us some clues." Katie was already looking forward to her new project.

As Katie picked up the treasures, a small picture dropped onto the floor. She picked it up to take a closer look. A handsome young soldier in full Army uniform looked back at her. His hair was cut in a military-style crewcut. His eyes carried the impression of an impish spirit, and his facial expression implied the presence of a hidden smile. Apparently, he wasn't supposed to look happy in an official military photograph. His castle-type insignia indicated he served in the United States Army Corps of Engineers. His rank was Lieutenant, but she couldn't tell from the black-and-white photo whether he was a First or Second Lieutenant.

"He doesn't look like anyone I know, although he does

resemble Gramps a little. He has the same faint trail of freckles over his nose that Gramps had."

Intrigued by the young man's photo, Katie turned it over and read the message on the back: *"You'll just have to be content to hold this picture 'til I get back. All my love, Chaz."* It was dated 1942. "He must have been very special to Gram. I wonder who he was. We know it's not Gramps—his name was Joe."

Laura Katherine took the picture from Katie. "This might be Gramps' brother, Charles--he said they called him 'Chaz.' He was killed in France during World War II and is buried in a military cemetery there."

Katie vaguely remembered family references to Uncle Charles, but she hadn't paid attention to what her grandfather said about him back then.

Laura Katherine continued her trip down Memory Lane. "My mother said she was named for him. Her name was Charlotte Katherine, but everyone called her *Lottie*."

"What? I never knew your mother's first name was Charlotte," Katie interjected. "She was always just Aunt Lottie to me!"

Suddenly, a shiver of recognition shook Katie's shoulder. "Oh, my gosh! Gramps' brother's name was Charles, and your mother was named after him. The picture's inscription sounds like he loved Gram and knew she would be waiting for his return from the war."

Katie picked up the envelope in her lap. "The picture fell out of this. Maybe the letter inside will give us more details." Katie noticed the French postmark in the right-hand corner of the envelope. She carefully unfolded the letter and read its message out loud.

My dearest Kat,

I arrived at my new assignment yesterday, but I can't tell you where I am—security, you know. All I can say is it's a foreign country, and I don't speak the language. Maybe I'll learn a few phrases like, "Where's the nearest restaurant?"

My trip across the ocean on the military transport ship was long, uncomfortable, and uneventful. I think I'm grateful for that. The weather was good, the sky was vivid blue, and the water was smooth. Water, water everywhere for this country boy!

I've had a lot of time to think about you and the plans we're making for our life together when this war is over. Remember that little display table we bought at a flea market? You said those spindly legs looked like mine. HA! That table can be a symbol of our future—the first piece of furniture for the first house we will live in together. Just think, we can pass it down from generation to generation and keep it in our family forever.

I constantly look at your picture so I'm enclosing my official military "mug shot" for you to keep close to your heart while I'm gone. I'm already counting the days until I return to you.

The war going on around me is scary, but I'll try to stay out of harm's way. I know I don't have to ask you to pray for me—you started doing that before I left!

They just announced chow call, so I have to end this. I sure don't want to miss any meals.

All my love,

Chaz

The cousins exchanged glances as Katie finished reading the letter. "Imagine that! *Kat* must have been his nickname for Gram. They were in love and planned to marry when he returned from the war. His letter explains why the table was so important to Gram, but where does Gramps fit into these revelations?" The women looked at each other with a question that was too incredible to express out loud.

As Katie returned the letter to its original place, her fingers touched an object hidden in the corner of the envelope. She pulled out a small brass ring.

"Look, Laura Katherine, it's another hidden treasure."

She took the ring from Katie's hand. "I've seen rings like this at carnivals and state fairs. People used them as game tokens. They don't have any value."

"I can't find an explanation of its significance," Katie mused. "It's too small to be a wedding ring. I wonder why Gram kept it."

Laura Katherine looked at the heirloom table. "Maybe she kept it as a symbol of their future, like the table." She returned the ring to Katie so she could put it with the letter.

As Katie dropped the ring into its designated place, she looked at the picture of Uncle Charles again and wondered what it meant. "In my imagination, I see Uncle Charles getting down on one knee at the State Fair. He offers the ring to Gram in a mock proposal." Katie chuckled at her imagined scenario. "Well, it *could* have happened that way." Laura Katherine just shook her head as Katie rambled on about the ring.

Katie persisted with her theory. "We'll probably never know for certain why a token brass ring was among Gram's significant memories, but I like my version!"

After a long pause, Katie voiced the *elephant in the room* question. "Do you suppose Gram was pregnant with your mother when Uncle Charles went to France? Maybe your mom was actually Uncle Charles' child."

Laura Katherine was quiet as she considered Katie's question. "I guess that's possible. If a situation like that happened in those days, a close male relative often stepped up, married the girl, and claimed the child as his own. People might have suspected the truth, but no one ever acknowledged it publicly. None of our relatives who would know for sure are still living."

Katie added her logic to Laura Katherine's answer. "Gramps was a good man, so he might have married our grandmother and considered your mother as his own biological child. Do you think there's more significance to the name *Charlotte* than just a derivative of his brother's name?"

Katie gave a slight shiver. "Oh! I just got chills!"

Laura Katherine considered Katie's response. "I know Gram and Gramps loved each other, and they had a strong marriage. Surely, Gramps is truly my grandfather."

Katie looked at the next discovery from the middle drawer of the *Katherine* table." She held a delicate newspaper clipping, yellowed with age. Her hands shook slightly as she tried to smooth out the folds in the fragile paper. "This must be Uncle Charles' obituary. We have to get it laminated before it disintegrates completely." She read the notice to Laura Katherine.

A funeral service for Charles Robert McDaniel will be held at 2 o'clock on February 19, 1943, at Calvary Baptist Church in Conway, Arkansas, as a memorial marker is placed at the family plot. Lt. McDaniel died in combat in the region of Lorraine, France, where his body remains. He is survived by his parents, William and Katherine McDaniel, and his brothers, Joseph and William, Jr. He will be given a full military salute in honor of his sacrifice. After the service, family and friends are invited to gather at the church to share their memories of Charles.

Through the years, her father, Bill, had told Katie about his family's visits to the gravesites of the McDaniel family. She wished she had paid more attention to his memories.

At that moment, Katie's stomach gave an audible growl. "This is more information than I can handle on an empty stomach. Let's take a lunch break."

Reluctantly, the cousins left the *Katherine* table and went into the kitchen to focus their attention on Katie's table. She went to the refrigerator and proudly removed a plate of sliced, juicy red tomatoes carefully arranged in a circle on Gram's Spode China. "These are fresh off the vines in my garden. I picked them this morning."

Katie returned to the refrigerator and took out a vintage glass bowl filled with chicken salad. "I used Gram's recipe—the one with the pecans, grapes, and pineapple. I also baked a fresh peach pie for dessert. That was Gramps' favorite, remember?" They smiled at the shared memory of Gram's skill in the kitchen as Katie served the nostalgic luncheon. They could feel the magnetism of the *Katherine* table as they ate.

After cleaning up the kitchen, they resumed their positions on the comfy cushions in the living room. Laura Katherine looked at their scattered treasures and exhaled a long breath.

"I remember when Gram and Gramps took that trip to France to celebrate their 50th wedding anniversary. They said they were going to visit Uncle Charles' grave. Gramps said visiting his brother's grave was on his *bucket list*. They were excited about the trip, but I remember seeing a small tear inching its way down Gram's cheek. Maybe a visit to his brother's grave was more than just a bucket list item for Gramps."

"I remember when they took that trip. It meant so much to both of them," Katie recalled.

"The pictures they brought back were amazing. Gram kept them in her table's middle drawer."

Laura Katherine's expression indicated she had journeyed back in time to a revealing conversation with Gramps.

"He said the cemetery was larger than he expected. The pictures showed hundreds of white crosses perfectly aligned on a beautiful hillside. It looked so peaceful." Katie joined Laura Katherine in her time-travel.

"Gramps explained the significance of the cemetery. He said it was comforting to know that his brother's gravesite would have perpetual care. It's maintained by the American Battle Monuments Commission in Washington, DC. I didn't know the United States had an agency like that until he told me."

Laura Katherine continued with another revelation from that

conversation. "Gramps said that several years after the war, the family was given the opportunity to bring Uncle Charles' body back to Arkansas, but they decided to leave it in France. His marker in the Conway Cemetery was enough of a reminder for them."

"I wonder why." Katie was puzzled at the decision. "I think I would have chosen to bring him home so we could visit his grave."

Laura Katherine gazed out the window. "That's what I thought too, so I asked him. According to Gramps, they left Uncle Charles' remains in France because people from all over the world would visit that cemetery, see his name, and know of his sacrifice for his country. On the other hand, only family and friends would know of his service if they brought his body back to Arkansas. He said his brother wasn't in either place; but this way, his memory would be honored in both places."

Katie pondered the family's decision and wondered what she would have done. She picked up the obituary and reread it. "That must have been a hard decision, but now I have a better understanding of why they made that choice."

Katie put on her "detective hat" and was ready to share her conclusions with Laura Katherine. "Okay, let's think about what we have so far. We know the young man in the picture is Gramps' brother, Charles. He was killed during World War II, and is buried in a military cemetery in Lorraine, France. He was very special to Gram, and they planned to marry after the war. That's probably why Gram kept the brass ring. The *Katherine* table was the first piece of furniture they bought for their future home--that's why Gram insisted that it stay in the family for all these years. The lingering question is whether Uncle Charles is your mother's biological father. After all, she *was* named for him."

Laura Katherine took the picture from Katie. "You're right. The picture, letter, ring, and obituary fit into Uncle Charles' story, but that doesn't mean he was my mother's biological father."

Katie's thoughts were consumed with finding out Laura Katherine's true heritage, so she wasn't listening. "I think we could find that out fairly easily. There has been extensive research done on DNA identification, so we can find out the process and go from there."

Katie was eager to begin this new adventure. There were so many avenues they could take to jump-start their research.

Laura Katherine silently stared at the table as Katie speculated. With a frown, she finally said, "Calm down Katie! You're assuming that I want to know that information, but I don't."

"Of course, you want to know, Laura Katherine! Aren't you curious?"

"Think about it, Katie, what difference does it make who my biological grandfather is?"

Laura Katherine's tone was harsher than she had intended. "Gramps is the only grandfather I ever knew, and there was never any indication that Mama wasn't his biological child. I have read articles about DNA research too, but I like things the way they are. Of course, if a mysterious medical issue comes up in the future, I might change my mind. In the meantime, Gramps was Gramps and always will be. His name was Joe!"

Katie could tell by Laura Katherine's reaction that the discussion was over, so she settled back in her recliner, closed her eyes, and considered the events of the day.

I'll just have to be content with being the new owner of the Katherine table and not ask questions. For now, anyway...

THE LORD OF TIME

TINA MIDDLETON

"Shari, can you come here for a minute?"

A skitter of unease passed over Shari at the urgent tone of Chad's voice. She set down her book and stood behind her husband as he stared at the computer controlling the time machine. Shari leaned over to see the settings, and a heaviness settled over her. Someone had entered first-century Palestine as the destination. She stepped back and struggled to get the words past the tightness in her throat.

"You didn't set that?"

"No." Chad's terse answer sent chills down Shari's spine.

"Do you think Eddie…?" She couldn't finish. Surely, their friend wouldn't go back and try to change history. The three of them had been friends for several years, since their university days. Eddie had been Chad's best man at their wedding. Though not a believer, Eddie had always shown respect for Chad and Shari's faith. All three held a firm conviction that history was to be observed, not changed.

Shari swallowed her fear and faced Chad. "He knows the rules, Chad. The time machine is only for observation and research."

Even as she spoke, doubt rose like an ugly specter.

Chad nodded, his jaw tight as he spoke. "Don't you remember our discussion last night?"

They had stayed up late talking about Christianity and world history. Eddie had grown up in a worldly home and saw Jesus as a good man who had been a victim of first-century politics. He said he wished he could go back to that time and rescue Jesus from the crucifixion. Eddie believed that if Jesus had not been killed, He would have married and left an incredible legacy for all who came after Him. Chad and Shari firmly disagreed. The two shared a strong Christian heritage and knew how vital Christ's death and resurrection were. They explained to Eddie how important those events had been to world history but could not make him understand.

The three of them had argued about it until Eddie abruptly decided he was going to bed. The unfinished discussion still hung heavily in the air, and Shari wondered if they could have said anything else that might have convinced their friend. She saw in Chad's eyes the same question as well as something else - Guilt. Before he said a word, Shari knew what was coming.

"Shari, I have to go after him. Maybe I can catch him before he does something stupid."

"Chad, you don't always have to be the one to fix things. God does not need your help to manage world events."

She laid her hand on his jaw and looked into his eyes. Her words were firm, but her eyes overflowed with love.

Chad laid his hand on hers and swept a light kiss across her fingers. He released her hand and went to their room, where he grabbed a suitcase and began throwing clothes into it.

"I have to go. The time machine is my creation. My responsibility."

Shari grabbed his arm, slowing him and getting him to look at her. Frustration crept into her voice. "The time machine is *our* creation and responsibility. Besides, if he had done what he talked about, history would already be changed."

Chad shook his head. "I don't know. Maybe there's a delay or something." He stopped and stared at the suitcase. "What am I doing? I can't take this with me."

He pulled Shari into his arms and cradled her there for a long moment. Shari didn't know if he was comforting her or trying to draw it from her. She felt him tremble as he released her.

"Shari, I have to do this." He tucked a strand of blonde hair behind her ear.

Her blue eyes filled with tears.

"Pray for me," he whispered. She nodded and watched him stride into the workroom and step into the time machine. Before he closed the door, he gazed into Shari's eyes.

"I'll bring him back," he promised.

Eddie stared in wonder at the surrounding sights. He had always wanted to visit the Holy Land. Now he was here—right in the center of human history.

The young engineer inspected himself to make sure he looked inconspicuous. The time machine adjusted whatever they were wearing to the clothing of the time they were visiting. He wore the rough robe of a common laborer. Eddie checked the small patch of cloth and electronics affixed to the back of his neck. The language patch enabled him to understand the people he would interact with and speak their language.

"You there!"

Eddie looked up to see a burly man leading a donkey and her colt coming toward him. The man slapped the donkey's lead into Eddie's hands.

"Make yourself useful and watch these for me."

The big man leaned closer, his grizzled face a few inches from Eddie's. "Make sure nothing happens to them. I am sure I would have no trouble finding you."

He turned to leave after making sure Eddie had a firm hold on the donkey's rope. Eddie stared after the man, then turned to study the two animals. The donkey nibbled at the grass on the side of the road while her colt stared back at Eddie.

Now, what do I do? I need to find Jesus, but I'm stuck here donkey-sitting!

Eddie snorted in disgust as he tied the donkey to a nearby date tree. He glanced up to see two young men walking toward him. One was bearded and seemed the older of the two. The younger one raised his hand in greeting while the older one reached for the rope.

"Wait! You can't take those! They belong…"

"The Master needs to use your donkey and her colt." The man's expression remained impassive but firm as he led the animal away.

It was a statement, not a request. At first, Eddie resented the man's tone. Who did this guy think he was? Then he realized this was the donkey that Jesus would ride into Jerusalem! He had arrived at just the right time and place. Awe swept over him as he thought about how the events had fallen into place.

Eddie followed the men down the street and addressed his question to the younger man. He wore a more open and friendly expression than the man who took the donkey.

"May I come too?"

The younger man smiled at him and beckoned with his free hand. "Come, I will take you to the Master."

They fell in step with each other, and Eddie's new acquaintance turned to him, the friendly grin still on his face. "I am Andrew. The man with me is my brother, Simon. What is your name?"

"My name is Edward, but my friends call me Eddie."

"Eddie." Andrew tried the name and laughed.

"It sounds unusual, but I like it. Have you ever met the Master before?"

Eddie shook his head as he felt his way through the conversation. He had to be careful to not give away where he was from, or *when* he was from. "Not yet. But I would like to meet Him. I've heard a lot, uh, much about Him."

Simon and Andrew cast curious glances at their new friend. "Your speech is strange."

Eddie held back a grin. The language patch was an engineering marvel, but it had some quirks. One was the inability to change the user's dialect or accent. Thus, Eddie's Aramaic had a distinctly American southern accent.

Simon looked suspiciously at their guest, but Andrew clapped his brother on the shoulder. "That's what some people say about us."

Eddie hurried to get the attention off himself. "Why do they say that about you?"

"We're from Galilee, like the Master." Andrew's voice held a note of pride about coming from the same region as Jesus.

The three approached a group surrounding a man who was instructing them. He seemed ordinary - brown hair, brown eyes, and olive skin. Nothing stood out about him until Eddie looked into his eyes. They overflowed with love and compassion. But there was something else, and Eddie searched his mind for the right word. *Power! Yes, this simple, ordinary man exuded a holy power.*

"Welcome, Edward. We're glad you could join us."

Eddie blinked. Although no one had introduced him, Jesus knew his name already. He glanced at the other men, then back at Jesus, and saw Him warmly watching. Eddie wondered if Jesus knew why he was there. He felt a shiver of—what was it? Anxiety? Fear? Excitement?

The men helped Jesus onto the donkey and led the animal

toward Jerusalem. Crowds began to gather as the large group of disciples lifted their voices to shout and sing.

"Hosanna! Hosanna to the King! Blessed is He who comes in the name of the Lord."

Many cut palm leaves from nearby trees and placed them on the road. Some took off their cloaks for the same purpose. It was exhilarating, and Eddie found himself caught up in the crowd's enthusiasm.

He watched the people surrounding Jesus and singing praises to Him. He saw the man who had left the donkeys in his care. The owner's eyes widened when he noticed the two animals and their caretaker. Eddie thought the man would confront them, but he turned to his neighbor and pointed proudly to the donkey.

"That's *my* animal! I thought the Master might need a good, sturdy beast to carry Him, so I was happy to loan Him mine."

Eddie shook his head in wonder. The adoration and love flowing from the crowds overwhelmed him. Surely these people were the ones to help him stop the Jewish authorities and the Romans when the time came.

Chad paused to collect and orient himself. He was dressed in a worn, brown tunic and sandals. As he stood observing his surroundings, he heard shouting and singing. He must be near Jerusalem at the time of Jesus' triumphal entry. But where was Eddie? Was he in Jerusalem too? Was he caught up in the celebration as the Messiah entered the holy city?

The singing captured Chad's attention, drawing him quickly in its direction. He had to find Eddie and persuade him to return to their time before he attempted to rescue Jesus. Chad felt the weight of the world on him. What if he failed? Would the world come to an end? Would it be stuck in a primitive state? Chad knew many of the advances made in history were because of Christian men and women who served God by exploring and doing great things. Would everything come to a halt?

Shari's words came back to him in a gentle reminder. "You don't always have to be the one to fix things."

They had discussed this on multiple occasions. In fact, Shari had challenged him about his lack of faith in God's sovereignty.

"God is in control," she often reminded him. "He doesn't need your help."

Chad knew she was right, but he felt responsible not only for his own actions, but also for what others did if it was because of something Chad had done, like creating the time machine. If he had not presented the idea to his wife and friend, they would not have made it, or gone back in time to observe and learn, or tried to go back to change history, like Eddie had done.

Eddie watched in disbelief as the crowd screamed for Jesus's crucifixion. This was the same group who had sung his praises just a few days before.

After the procession into Jerusalem, Eddie had stayed with the disciples. He felt he was just beginning to learn that there was so much more to Jesus than merely a good man, teacher, or healer. The sorrow in Jesus' eyes as he gazed at the angry mob and listened to their hateful shouts twisted Eddie's heart.

Eddie snorted as he thought of his grand idea of rescuing Jesus. Even if he had a sword, he couldn't take on the soldiers or the crowd. The weight of his foolishness brought him to tears.

Suddenly, someone bumped into Eddie from behind and grabbed his tunic. Eddie jumped and instinctively pulled back his fist to fight him off. However, just before he punched his assailant, he got a better look at him.

Chad!

The words burst from Eddie's mouth as he gaped in disbelief. "What are you doing here?"

Before his time with Jesus, Eddie's response would have been to get angry at Chad for following him, but the past week had changed him. He understood more about Jesus now. Eddie grabbed his friend's hand, but Chad pulled away and grabbed Eddie's shoulders.

"I've been looking for you. Please, Eddie, don't try to change what happens here. You will change world history."

Eddie contemplated the scene. Jesus stood before Pontius Pilate. Somehow, even in the face of certain death, Jesus' face was calm. The Jewish religious leaders poured their insults and abusive language on Him and demanded Pilate crucify Him. The disciples who had followed Him so faithfully now hid at the back of the crowd, frightened and ashamed. Eddie hung his head, and tears rolled down his cheeks.

"I get what you're saying, Chad. I really do, but somehow, it still seems so unfair. So wrong. Why does Jesus have to die?"

Chad pulled him into a tight hug, tears running down his face.

"I know, bud. It's hard to understand." He indicated the procession wending its way out of Jerusalem and turned his steps in to follow. "Come on, we're here now, so we might as well watch the whole thing."

The two friends followed the agonizing procession to Golgotha. The smell of death filled the air. In sorrow and wonder, they watched as the soldiers nailed Jesus to the wooden beams of the cross and raised it up until it settled with a jolt. They saw him writhe in pain yet still forgive those who inflicted that pain on him. Both of them knew that they had caused him pain as well.

When darkness overtook the skies, the two friends turned to each other. Reading about the crucifixion was one thing. To actually be there and experience the darkness and grief was something they knew they would always remember. When they heard Jesus's final words from the cross, their hearts filled with overwhelming sadness and the young men sobbed.

After Jesus's body was taken down, Chad and Eddie turned and left the site of death. Chad laid his hand on Eddie's shoulder, his face still drawn with grief. "We need to go home now."

Eddie shook his head. "I don't think so. I think we're supposed to stay a few more days."

Chad cocked his head as he studied his friend. "Why?"

"I can't explain it." Eddie turned to view the hill that stood bare now, the crosses removed and the crowd scattered. "I feel like there's something more we need to wait for."

Eddie and Chad camped outside of Jerusalem for the next two days. They discussed what they had seen and heard and their experiences over the past week. Eddie tried to convey what he had learned while walking with Jesus. He wanted Chad to know he was a different man from the one who had declared his intention to rescue Jesus.

Sunday morning dawned clear and cool. A sense of expectancy hung in the air as they stood and gazed at the gates of the holy city and the surrounding countryside.

Suddenly, there was a disturbance in the garden where Jesus had been laid in a borrowed tomb. Two Roman soldiers hurried toward the temple; their faces white with fear. A few minutes later, a group of women came rushing along the path, chattering excitedly among themselves.

Eddie and Chad's eyes widened as they heard the women's conversation.

"He's alive! We saw Him!"

Eddie turned to Chad, his eyes shining with hope. "We can leave now," he proclaimed. "That's what we were waiting for."

Chad nodded, though his heart felt heavy with conviction. He had come to rescue his friend and to try to save the world. Now he realized how right Shari was and how foolish he had been. God did not need Chad to save the world. He sent Jesus to do that. Chad wanted to be alone and confess his sin of pride and desire to control everything.

Before he could move, he saw a Man in white robes appear before him and Eddie. His eyes widened in awe. The risen Christ stood before them. His voice flowed like warm honey over Chad's aching heart as His words strengthened and affirmed.

"Eddie, I am so glad you have chosen to believe in Me. Go and be My witness at home and abroad."

"Chad, though a caring and responsible man, you have tried to take on burdens that are not yours to bear. I am sovereign and will show what *you* need to do and what needs to be trusted to *Me*. Soon you and Shari will have a family. Share with them the heritage of faith and know that My love and power are the same throughout time. I am the Lord of life and the Lord of time."

Chad and Eddie opened their eyes to find a worried Shari standing over them.

"I thought you two would never wake up after staying up so late last night. Come see the time machine. It's changed somehow."

The two men stumbled from their couches and across the workroom. The time machine stood in its place, and the men shook their heads in puzzlement at Shari's words. Then they saw it.

On the side of the machine, etched in golden holographic lines, glowed a picture of a cross. Next to it stood a cave with the stone rolled away. Below the etching, three simple words filled them with wonder.

"Jesus is Lord."

THE HANDOFF

CALVIN HUBBARD

Seeing that we are surrounded...

om felt hemmed in. The stress of the unfinished tasks before him more than offset the relief of getting a few tasks done. The self-imposed pressure about the upcoming meeting squeezed him more than the buoyant confidence he had in knowing the material. All this made Tom feel like he was wearing a scuba suit that was three sizes too small. Taking in a long, deep breath, Tom exhaled slowly and leaned back in his chair. He looked around his office just to get his eyes off the two computer monitors he'd been staring at for the last hour. It's not that he hadn't made progress on the task at hand. He had. But the progress did not supply the relief he wanted...or needed. He just needed to hit the pause button.

He scanned the room as he took another deep breath. He ran his hands through his dark hair streaked with gray, as he often did when he was tired. His eyes caught the gold lettering on the spine of the first book on the shelves lining the office. Closing his eyes, he could see the book cover in his mind—hardback, black marbling imprinted on the red covers, gray spine. Tom stood up, reaching to the top shelf and took the book off the shelf. Without opening it, he could visualize pages within its covers -- pictures, line drawings, italicized print, and short articles with enough information to satisfy, or to ignite, a curious mind. Holding the book in his hands, Tom returned to his chair and, in his mind, returned to another place and time.

Tom found himself at his mom's parents' home. The asbestos siding shone in the light of a mid-morning sun. Tom, two of his siblings, Josh and Mikayla, and his parents had just arrived at Mamaw and Papaw White's house after a two-hour drive. Everyone got out of the blue, four-door Ford Galaxie 500 and headed to the house. Josh opened the gate to the yard, and everyone walked up the gray concrete sidewalk that cut the vibrant green lawn that led to the front door.. The house was surrounded with various shrubs, full of blooming flowers. The buzz of bees flying from one flower to another filled the air. The porch, spanning the whole width of the house, was a welcome place with a swing at the right edge and three wooden rocking chairs waiting to be used.

The buzz of conversations filled the inside of the house. Some of Tom's aunts, uncles, and cousins also had come to Mamaw's and Papaw's house. Hugs and handshakes were exchanged. Then the men found a place to sit and discuss sports, politics, or swap fish stories. The women headed to the kitchen to help Mamaw finish preparing lunch, catch up on family news, and set the dining room table. Some of the cousins went outside to chat, to play hide-and-seek, or to throw rocks from the gravel drive into the woods. Tom didn't know what they did. He was too young to go with his high-school-aged cousins. Other cousins walked to the back of the house where all the empty Coke bottles were. They'd pick up a bottle, turn it over, and read where the bottle was made and filled. Today, he didn't feel like looking at Coke bottles.

Instead, he loitered in the living room with his dad, uncles, and grandfather.

Tom didn't pay attention to the men's conversations. Looking around the living room, he spied a hardback book. It was a big, thick, heavy-looking book. It had black marbling imprinted on a red hardback cover, a gray spine with gold piping, and gold letters. He asked, "Papaw, may I read that book there?"

"Sure, son," was his grandfather's reply. *Strange Stories, Amazing Facts* read the spine and the cover. What strange stories would be told? What amazing facts would be discovered?

The sounds of the conversations around Tom faded like a soundman lowering the PA system at a concert to zero. A tunnel began to form on the edges of Tom's vision. All he could see were the words, the pictures, the color prints, the black-and-white photographs, the line art, and reproductions of woodcuts. Space was explored; science was explained; art was unveiled; futurists forecasted the future. Each time Tom and his family visited, Tom was content to turn the pages of this book, reading new stories and rereading familiar stories, both of which were filling his thirst for knowledge and firing his curiosity.

Tom's desire to keep drinking from the fountain of knowledge in this book prompted him one time, as he and his family were leaving to go home, to boldly ask his grandfather, "Papaw, may I have this book?"

Tom's mother quickly replied, "Tom, it's rude to ask for that book."

As Tom flushed with embarrassment, Papaw White said, "Lucy, it's okay." Then, looking Tom in the eye, Papaw White said, "Son, the book is yours."

...by so great a cloud of witnesses...

The memory of that day at Mamaw and Papaw White's house

faded. Tom was back in his office. Returning that book to its place, he looked to his left and saw another book. This one wasn't in as good a shape as *Strange Stories, Amazing Facts.* The maroon spine had come off years before, exposing the ocher-colored paper that helped hold the pages of this 1,000-page book together. As before, Tom could visualize the cover—a gold American flag waving above the gold lettering of the title that was placed between two gold horizontal lines.

Tom now found himself back in his childhood home, sitting in the living room. The ceiling light and the lamp on the corner table illuminated the room. The TV wasn't on, as Tom's dad read another one of the western novels he enjoyed. His mom was crocheting another afghan for one of the grandchildren. Tom himself sat at the end of the couch with this large, maroon-covered book in his lap. He, as he had done many times before, had pulled the book off the shelf in the closet where the family library was kept and started flipping through the pictures. Tom loved looking at the pictures, letting the pictures tell the stories instead of the words of the chapters on the already yellowed pages. The pictures were black-and-white but were full of action, energy, and story. From his elementary school years through his high school years, Tom perused this book. From time to time, he would read a chapter here and a chapter there. Before graduating high school, Tom made up his mind to read this tome cover to cover. He was proud of himself when he did so.

From those yellowed pages, Tom learned the political and military aspects of the Second World War. He saw the movers and shakers of the political and military powers. He envisioned the soldiers involved in service, the airmen manning the aircraft flying over occupied Europe while making their bombing runs or flying from aircraft carriers in the Pacific campaign.

Remembering this book made Tom think of a picture of three young men that hung in his home. These men were dressed in the uniforms of the United States Army Air Force. Two of the men, identical twins, were on either side of their older brother. Tom recalled that he always had trouble telling which one of the twins was his dad, as the twins looked so much alike.

When Tom's dad died, his siblings knew that this history book, along with several other books from the family library, would go to Tom. All of Tom's siblings told him, "Brother, the book is yours."

...let us run with endurance the race set before us...

As that memory faded and Tom again found himself in his office, he turned his head back to the right, and his eyes fell upon a small, red-leather-covered Bible. It was the smallest of the three books that he focused upon. This time, he found himself in a now long-closed Christian bookstore. He was standing beside his fiancée, who was buying Tom his first study Bible. He recalled what she had written on the presentation page. Then another memory replaced the memory of the purchase. It was a memory about that presentation page. It wasn't what was written but *when* it was written. Tom didn't realize until a few years later that El had given him this Bible on the first anniversary of his dad's death. The feelings of that moment of realization came back as if it occurred at that moment. It made this Bible special. It exponentially added personal value to that Bible. Tom reached out from his chair and pulled this Bible off the shelf. He opened it to the presentation page and looked again at the date El wrote. Tom was still amazed that he hadn't noticed this when she bought and gave him this Bible. "Tom, this book is yours."

Tom leaned forward in his chair, once again aware of his surroundings—his two computer screens shining, a small fan humming as it circulated air, the sun shining through the window, warming the room. He looked to his right and saw his shelves full of books. He turned around and saw another set of shelves full of books. He turned back around, facing his computer, and looked left to see another set of shelves full of books. Tom noticed books given to him by pastors, by family, by fellow-church members, and by friends. He noticed two books published around 1810, as well as books published this year. His library spanned years and generations. Tom realized he was surrounded by a great cloud of witnesses, giving him a heritage measured by a hunger for knowledge, for righteousness and justice, for hope. His was a heritage of wisdom and knowledge handed to him like a baton in a relay race through the generosity of family and friends. Appreciation arose for his grandfather handing off the book that ignited curiosity in him. Appreciation arose for his father's love of history that ignited his own desire to learn history. Appreciation arose for his fiancée, now his wife, who shared her personal faith, a faith borne through the writings of men who lived millennia ago, writing what and living how the Holy Spirit directed them. The books Joe gave him jump-started his personal library. The books Jim gave him helped him be a better student of the Scriptures. "I am rich indeed," thought Tom, "and I hope I, too, will handoff what I've received from my grandfather, my father, my friends and my faith, a good and godly heritage that spans generations."

"Therefore we also, since we are surrounded by so great a cloud of witnesses, let us lay aside every weight, and the sin which so easily ensnares us, and let us run with endurance the race that is set before us, looking unto Jesus, the author and finisher of our faith, who for the joy that was set before Him endured the cross, despising the shame, and has sat down at the right hand of the throne of God." (Hebrews 12:1–2, NKJV)

CROSSING COHAY BRANCH

MARY LOU CHEATHAM

Grandma died. She left no doubts among her children still on earth—six daughters and one son—about where she went...straight to heaven. What she did leave, though, was a home full of stuff, eighty acres, and the old shack she used to live in—the one where she raised her children. Neither of the two structures had ever seen a lick of paint. Why would anybody who didn't live on the highway bother to paint a house?

The Sunday afternoon came when the sisters and brother planned to divide and take her personal property from the new residence—the one where she lived—a modern home without a dogtrot. It had windows with glass panes too. I used to love the windows at the old shack. They were all wood and attached to hinges.

After Sunday morning church and potluck dinner at Aunt Rose's house, all us kids dressed in tee-shirts, pedal pushers or cutoff jeans, and flip-flops. We ate three messes of fried chicken, Aunt Kate's butterbeans and dumplings, my mama's blackberry cobbler, and Aunt Ida's stuffed eggs. All so good. We cleaned up, and the whole family walked through Aunt Rose and Uncle Bully's pasture to the place where Grandma had lived. It didn't take long for folks to start sorting the stuff.

On the porch stood my cousin Becca, holding two paper bags. "Come on, Molly. We got to get on with this. Tote your sack. Let's go."

I took my bag and didn't ask where.

"Let's go to Grandma's shed and take two of her walking sticks in case we see a snake."

A lump lodged in my throat. "I hope not."

Becca stuck her head inside the back door and told the adults a half-truth about her plan. "We're going to play."

"It don't matter. No one's listening," I said. We were old enough to take care of ourselves.

Down the path toward the old shack, we went. Becca led the way. "If we see anything interesting, I'll draw a picture of it." She turned toward me. "Molly, you can write about it."

At the end of the bitterweed field, the path dropped to a low place where one of the many branches of Cohay Creek cut through the drop-offs in its mad rush to Leaf River. Teacher said all that water was on its way to the Gulf.

When we reached the bottom of the holler, we heard a mournful wail that would make every hair on your body stand up. The cry sounded like an old woman screaming in the distance.

Becca grabbed my arm and shook it. "You hear that?"

"Yep. It's the panther."

Becca shivered all over. "You scared?"

"No." I stuck out my chin. "You?"

She shook her head. "No way. Grandma used to say the panther hangs around the branch to eat other critters."

"That's right." I nodded. "She's got lots of things to eat besides little girls."

We'd heard the panther's distant cry all our lives. We'd never seen her, though. Becca said, "My mama told me the panther ain't nearly as far away as she sounds. We better keep our eyes open."

I studied the path. "We got to find the shallow place where it's easy to cross the branch."

We took off our flip-flops and put them in our paper sacks. The clear cold water washed over sand and rocks.

As we waded through the branch, I felt the lump in my throat again. "Watch for water moccasins."

As soon as we crossed the branch, we slipped our feet back into our flip-flops.

Becca was on a mission. "Come on, Molly."

I had my ideas about what she was doing, even though I wasn't sure. "Becca, what's up?"

"Don't talk out loud. Try to keep your flip-flops from flopping." She led the way up the path toward the old dog-trot shack. When we reached the chinquapin tree at the edge of the clearing, a '46 or '47 dark gray Ford sat parked in front. "She's home."

"Who?"

"Cousin Julene." Becca dropped to the ground and sat cross-legged.

"Make sure you ain't sitting on an ant bed." I sat nearby. "It's about time you told me what we're doing."

Becca opened her tablet. "Julene lives in the old place. Grandma told me. She made me promise not to tell Mama or anybody. We've got to leave Julene a note."

"Oh, I see. Tell her to move."

"Right."

We wrote our notes. *Julene, you got to move out of here.*

We needed to hurry in case she saw us sitting on the ground out front. And what if our mothers didn't see us playing outside Grandma's new house? If they had to stop to go looking for us, they'd be madder than a wet hen.

Our notes folded in our hands, we sneaked up to the front porch. There, we stacked a rock on top of them.

Having done what we set out to do, we stood up. The door on the left side of the dogtrot squeaked. When it cracked open, a gun barrel poked through.

Becca was the one that started this, and now she shook all over.

A voice hollered from inside. "Get off my property!"

Becca spoke in a trembly voice. "It ain't your property."

The door flung open, and out stepped a woman with dark red curly hair sticking out all over her head. Her sunken eyes and splotched skin made her look wild. She wore a stained print dress and brogans.

"Name's Julene." Then she laughed, showing gaps in her brown teeth. "I know you young'uns. Becca and Molly. Y'all's grandma showed me your pictures."

She stepped closer, and we backed away. Becca was taller than me although she was a year younger. She hid behind me and grabbed my waist.

"You call her grandma." When Julene shook her head, the red curls went crazy. "I call her Aunt Jane."

My voice was so weak I didn't know whether she heard me. "Pleased to meet you."

It was what Mama had taught me to say because it was polite. Somehow though, it didn't sound right to say to Julene.

"I'm sure you are." Julene walked from the dogtrot to the edge of the front porch and leaned over. When she spit, a wad of snuff juice went into the yard. "Y'all's folks is too highfalutin to claim me. Aunt Jane she said I could live here though 'cause I didn't have no place to stay."

I hated to be the one to tell her, and yet we needed to be sure she knew Grandma had passed away. "Grandma died. Our folks is cleaning out her residence."

Becca stepped out from behind me. "You've got to leave quick."

116

Julene bent over toward Becca. "Now, why have I got to leave quick?"

I could feel how frightened Becca was, so I spoke. "Our mamas and aunts and uncle sold Grandma's property to Mr. Bennefield. He's gonna put a big lake here."

Julene frowned mean.

Why couldn't I make Julene understand? Becca helped me out. "He's fixing to bring in bulldozers and close this road. They'll tear down this house because the lake is going to be here. The old homeplace will be underwater. We're just trying to protect you."

Becca led the way, and I followed her as we eased toward the porch steps.

Julene took a pinch of fresh snuff from her can and stuck it in her mouth. She sounded funny when she talked with the wad behind her bottom lip. "When is this house going to be tore down?"

Both of us stopped and turned around. We answered at the same time. "Tomorrow."

We must've made her mad 'cause she reached for her rifle. "Git out of here before I shoot."

Toting Grandma's walking sticks and our tablets, we ran all the way to the chinquapin tree.

Becca and me was panting hard. I said, "We got to stop and catch our breath."

She looked around. "Julene might shoot, and we'll have to run."

I held my breath and let it blow slow out my nose. "If we don't get our wind, we won't be able to run."

As soon as we recovered, we crept down the path toward the branch crossing and stopped to take our flip-flops off.

On the other side, the panther stood. It had the fiercest looking eyes I'd ever seen, and them eyes zeroed in on us. Her shiny black fur told us nothing had ever defeated her. No scratches like she'd ever lost a fight. The most dangerous part of her was her powerful long legs. No doubt about it—she could have jumped across the branch and killed us with her claws and teeth.

We were goners. Becca fell and curled into a ball. She heaved with sobs.

I poked her back with my stick. "Get up, Becca. You're taller than me. I need your help."

Becca raised her head. "You're older."

"Honestly." I couldn't help feeling disgusted. "The panther doesn't know how old I am. She just knows you're bigger and taller."

Becca stood.

"Do what I tell you." I didn't know what I was talking about. I'd read something in a book. "Don't jump at her. Stand tall and look like a teacher. Hold your stick still beside you. Don't wave it at her."

Becca did as she was told, and I stood by her the same way.

I made my voice sound deep and loud but not unnatural. "We came down here to tell that woman in Grandma's old shack to move out. The problem is she wouldn't pay us no mind."

The panther jumped gracefully across the water and slinked our direction, but she didn't come no closer than six feet. As we watched, she sidestepped over onto the path toward Grandma's old home.

"Let's go." I crept to the shallow place where we crossed the branch, and Becca followed.

OUT OF THE DARKNESS

SUSAN HIERS FOSTER

I went to Maine to be inspired. Technically, my sister chose Maine for me. She's our family genealogical researcher, and I'm her assistant. How I got drafted for that unwanted job remains a mystery. It's hard to say no to my sister. She pestered me throughout the spring to travel to New England, wanting me to get rubbings off the tombstones of our maternal great-grandparents. They're buried in a cemetery outside Bangor, the area where the family settled after immigrating from Canada.

I was desperate, and it had nothing to do with my upcoming genealogical journey. My editor called weekly to check on my progress for a Christian devotional book I was writing. What was the problem with that? No progress. The dreaded writer's block held me in its grip. A trip to Maine would hopefully get my long-dormant creative juices flowing and, at the same time, appease my sister as I researched our ancestral history.

When my husband and I arrived in New England, Maine's beauty proved stunning. Solemn towers of majestic lighthouses overlooked rocky coasts as waves crashed. Screeching gulls swooped for their dinners. Plenty there to inspire, but I remained stagnant. Every evening at the hotel, I focused on my laptop's screen, which remained blank.

We had postponed the family sleuthing until the end of our getaway. Because of the famous horror writer Stephen King and our next-door neighbor Seth, I dreaded going to Bangor.

I like Seth. He's a good kid. Hard-working and dependable, the 12-year-old mows our lawn when we're out of town. He calls me "ma'am" and addresses my husband as "sir." Seth's passion is skateboarding. He whizzes down the sidewalk on his Santa Cruz board, a prized possession he bought with earnings from his neighborhood lawn business. Seth's thin frame leans into the wind. If he spots me or Mrs. Harper, his grandmother, watching from our adjoining yards, he flaps his arms as he sails past. Finishing with a flourish, the boy jumps the curb, his fingers gripping the board.

From my kitchen window, I occasionally see Seth reading on summer afternoons. Sprawled on his front porch swing, he's propped on stuffed pillows, balancing a book in his lap. I'm impressed that someone from his generation still reads real books and not stares at a digital device. Sometimes Seth's grandmother treats him to a bowl of popcorn. He munches as he gently rocks while Mrs. Harper relaxes in a wicker chair next to him. She thumbs through Reader's Digests or sometimes naps.

When I asked Seth about taking care of the yard while my husband and I visited Maine, he said there was no problem. But then the boy hesitated, looking down. Eventually, he peered up and asked if we were going to Bangor on our trip. I nodded yes. "Ma'am, would you do me a favor? Take a picture of Stephen King's house. He lives there, you know."

"You like Stephen King's books?" I don't know why I was surprised. Even though I admire King's writing style, I stay away from his books. Too dark for me. Even before I was a Christian, I never was a fan of creepy, ghoulish stuff. As a youngster, my sister (the one who still badgers me) would dare me to watch Twilight

Zone episodes or old sci-fi movies with her. I'd win the dare but later pay as I shivered in our old poster bed, peeking wide-eyed over the covers, my sister sleeping peacefully beside me.

"Sure, I like his books," my neighbor responded. "They're always exciting...plus, Stephen King and I have something in common."

"What's that?" What could Seth and the well-known author ever have in common?

The kid hesitated again. "He and I...both...have to sleep with the lights on."

———

So, there we were in Bangor. I looked through the bars of the tall black wrought-iron fence. The gate was topped with evil-looking bats and spiders. Stephen King's house. Closer to being a mansion, it was brick-red and resembled something out of a Hollywood set for an Addams Family movie. Only a menacing Dracula was missing, shrouded in gray mist, clasping a scrawled sign, "Visitors Beware."

Who could sleep in a house like that? Then I remembered what Seth said. I took a few pictures, then returned to our rental car. Other vehicles pulled up. Tourists scrambled out with their cell phone cameras, and then they dashed away.

We lingered. My husband worked the unfamiliar GPS, getting directions to the cemetery for my research. The eerie house held my gaze. For the first time, I noticed security cameras, and I didn't blame King. Kooky fans probably annoyed the heck out of the author and his family.

I wondered what it was like for Stephen King, once a 26-year-old high school English teacher, to compose a blockbuster first novel. That was just the beginning of a string of accolades lasting for decades.

But at what price? Would the writer trade his success to be able to sleep in the dark? I did not know, but I had enough to worry about, especially completing my own book. The deadline loomed at full speed.

Bam! Bam! Bam! Startled, we both jumped. Somebody pounded on the back windshield as I swung around. All I could see was a University of Maine navy blue T-shirt with two arms attached. I leaped out of the car and came close to colliding with...Stephen King.

He looked exactly how one expects Stephen King to look, rumpled and glasses crooked. "Hey, you guys planning to spend all day here? Sorry, folks, no autographs today," he said.

I wish we could have replied with at least one witty remark. Sadly, neither my husband (he told me later he assumed the guy was a security guard), nor I came up with anything remotely clever. My spouse said something about us leaving soon. I interrupted and asked, "Can I take a picture of you for my friend? It would mean so much to him."

Without a word, the author walked away. I called out, "The boy says he has trouble falling asleep in the dark...like you do." That stopped Stephen King. Cold. He turned and asked, "Why is that?"

"I don't know. Seth's my neighbor. Only 12," I responded. "He's the one who told me about you sleeping with the lights on." I cringed. The writer undoubtedly thought I was nosy, treading into his personal life he had no desire to discuss. Especially with a stranger.

"Doesn't matter the age," King said. "I was 14 when something awful happened. When I could stand it...and it took a long time...I turned it into a novella. Hardest thing I ever wrote. The trauma didn't go away. Unfortunately."

He fidgeted. I could tell King wanted to get back to his house. Then the writer shrugged and surprisingly said, "You can take my picture." He posed in front of the gruesome gate, even managing a lopsided half-smile. I thanked him and hurried back to the car. This time it was he who stopped me.

"About your friend...he probably only needs a sympathetic ear to listen. I would have appreciated confiding in someone. Who knows? It could have...maybe...even made a difference."

There was nothing more to say except, "Mr. King...Stephen? Would it be okay if I prayed for you? You know...about your trauma?" My voice trailed off. "If you don't mind?"

The writer's face shut down, his lips tight as we stared at each other. Slowly he raised his right hand. A thumbs up. With that, Stephen King retreated to his mansion, where the lights would burn through the long night.

I took King's advice when we returned home, but instead of talking to Seth, I went to his grandmother. Mrs. Harper was unaware something troubled her grandson, specifically his fear of the dark. She was anxious to talk to him.

The next day, Mrs. Harper dropped by my house. Over cups of coffee, she shared part of her grandson's painful conversation. Later, as Seth's grandmother was leaving, her eyes glistened with tears. I gave her the picture I had taken in Bangor, and she promised she would give it to Seth. Then we hugged goodbye.

In my study that evening, I silently thanked the author I had briefly met. Reaching for my prayer journal, I jotted down Seth's name—just below Stephen King's.

To the editor's delight and to my relief, the devotional book I was composing met its deadline...now with a new theme and title, *Intercessory Prayer for Those Who Live in Fear.*

.   .   .

"You will not be afraid of the terror by night," says the Lord. Psalm 91:5a (NAS)

I had not been back for long when my sister selected for me another traveling assignment. She had researched a small unknown town nestled in the Blue Ridge Mountains of Virginia, the birthplace of our paternal grandfather. As far as I know, no famous writers live there.

ABOUT PRISCILLA ADAMS

Priscilla Adams, known as Priscilla A., may be a little lady, but she has big dreams. Born in Shreveport, Louisiana, she always dreamed of becoming an actress, but God had so much more in store.

She is an accomplished writer, producer, actress, and film-maker, who has already had the pleasure of seeing her stories on the silver screen. Now she is making the pivot to putting her stories in book format.

She is on a course to tell stories that bring awareness to issues that face our world today in an entertaining and provocative format, reaching beyond your visual, beyond your mind, to your soul.

Her film projects include *Fate's Reunion*, *When I Needed You*, and her award-winning films *Reunited* and *High School Honeys*. Reunited secured a global distribution deal with Maverick Entertainment. More information is available on her website.

Connect with Priscilla Adams
Website: https://www.papvisions.com
Smashwords: https://www.smashwords.com/profile/view/
PriscillaAdams

ABOUT MARY LOU CHEATHAM

Mary Cooke, who signs her writing as Mary Lou Cheatham, grew up in Mississippi and moved to Louisiana in her twenties. Now she lives in west Texas.

As a child, Mary Lou Gregg allowed stories to roost in her head until they grew into novels, but she never completed any writing until she finished her second career. Living a busy life, she did not think she could spare minutes at the keyboard every day. Mary wrote some poems and short stories, which she always tossed into the trash can. When her life was the busiest ever, she could no longer suppress the desire to write. Experiences had shown her what she needed to say. The compulsion to tell her stories grabbed her and wouldn't let go. Every morning beginning at four o'clock, she spent two hours writing.

She grew up on a hill farm on the county line south of Taylorsville, Mississippi, and north of Hot Coffee. Her folks sat around the fireplace on winter nights with pecans to roast and shell, while they competed to see who could tell the most intriguing stories. On summer evenings, they sat on the front porch, where they shelled peas and beans while their parents told more tales. Sometimes they sat quietly and listened to the bobcats, owls, and whippoorwills.

The youngest of five children who lived to adulthood, she is the only survivor. One of her desires is to pass on a legacy to her nieces, nephews, and daughter. Writing a family memoir is a project she's working on. All her Gregg relatives and their acquaintances are welcome to send Mary anecdotes containing memories of the Gregg family to include in the book. So far, she has received some poignant and humorous stories.

All her life, curiosity has led her to read and study. In high school, she took every available subject and continued to take courses after earning her B. A. She attended five colleges in Mississippi.

She taught English and other subjects. When her daughter, Christie, was young, Mary worked part-time so she could spend as much time at home as possible. At the age of forty, she enrolled in the Louisiana Tech Nursing Program and two years later began working as a hospital RN.

After forty years with Robert Cheatham, a phenomenal trumpeter who taught at Louisiana Tech, where he inspired generations of great musicians before he died of a variant of a rare neuromuscular disease in 2002, Guillain Barré Syndrome, which seldom causes death, Mary spent more than a decade single and unattached.

Then she married John Cooke—a retired petroleum landman, history scholar with a degree from Emory, bird watcher, excellent cook, newshound, and faithful follower of Christ. They have a happy life. John has four grandchildren and four children with mates.

Now Christie lives in west Texas with her husband, Brandt. As a dairy nutritionist, Dr. Christie Underwood advises dairy farmers. Brandt, an agronomist, offers aid and advice to farmers challenged by a semi-arid climate.

In 2019, Mary and her husband, John, moved to Ransom Canyon, Texas, down the street from Christie and Brandt. John spent 2019 recovering from stage IV cancer. Mary and John are hiding from COVID-19—so far, successfully.

She writes. She goes to bed with a notebook and pen by her bed. The highlight of her day is the scheduled time she spends writing. When she can spare thirty minutes, she turns on her computer and spends three hours. Books about writing and about whatever subject she is researching clutter her personal space. Her thirst for ways to improve her craft has sent her to workshops and meetings with fellow writers. She reads mostly the works of fellow authors who have become her friends. She maintains her website, MaryLouCheatham.com.

She writes inspirational fiction with a bit of mystery, mostly historical but sometimes contemporary. Her writing always shows the oppressed, the downtrodden, and those mistreated by unkind human beings. A new novel about west Texas, *Deep from the Heart,* shines the light of God's love on a group of impoverished people ignored by their neighbors.

In 2020, she released *Letter from Belleau Wood,* which tells the story of young love during World War I and the 1918 influenza epidemic. Kirkus Reviews calls Mary Lou Cheatham's prose "compelling," also "textured and finely tuned to the time period and setting." Referring to *Letter from Belleau Wood,* Kirkus Reviews says, "Emotions involved are universal." Kirkus has selected this book to appear in a list called "Great Indie Books Worth Discovering."

Her readers delight in the way she goes deeply into her characters' emotions, often in historical settings. Reviewer Jonni Rich says Mary Lou's characters "endure tragedy and from tragedy seize all life has to offer them."

In 2021, she published *Beach Story,* a murder mystery with a romance involving a young woman with Asperger's.

Her latest book, a work of non-fiction, is an essential language reference called *Brilliant.* It is an anecdote-filled book designed to offer some entertaining insights into the English language and to help readers present their language in a more educated, brilliant manner.

You can receive a code that will allow you to get a free Audible book or receive her newsletter. Send her a message at Mary Cooke on Facebook.

Connect with Mary Lou Cheatham

Website: http://MaryLouCheatham.com
Blog: http://collardpatch.blogspot.com
Newsletter: https://mary-cooke.com/contact-mary
Smashwords: https://www.smashwords.com/profile/view/
MaryLouCheatham

Some of Mary Lou Cheatham's Books:

Covington Chronicles
Secret Promise
The Courtship of Miss Loretta Larson
The Dream Bucket
Manuela Blayne

Travelers in Painted Wagons on Cohay Creek (with Sarah Walker Gorrell)
House of Seven
Letter from Belleau Wood

Other Novels
Abi of Cyrene
As Doves Fly in the Wind
Deep from the Heart
Courage Is a Redhead
Lena's Hope
Beach Story

Anthologies
Coming of Age
With Words We Weave: Texas High Plains 2021 Anthology: Challenges
Second Changes

Children's Books
With Christie Marie Underwood
Bubba, the Firedog
Seth. the Shepard Boy
Brother Star, Sister Moon

Non-Fiction
Brilliant, Essential Language Reference

ABOUT BEVERLY FLANDERS

Beverly Flanders lives in Shreveport, Louisiana. She was born in Kokomo, Indiana, but spent a nomadic childhood as an Army brat. She has dabbled in various forms of writing since winning a poetry writing contest in junior high school. Her frequent moves and experiences living in different cultures and circumstances have given her plenty of material to develop into stories.

She graduated from Ferrum Junior College, Ferrum, Virginia, and attended Indiana University with the career goal of becoming a teacher. Those plans changed when she met her husband at IU, moved to Mansfield, Louisiana (her husband's hometown), and raised three perfect children. Those children went on to create strong, God-centered homes and six even more perfect grand-children.

Although she never became a *paid* professional, the opportunities to teach and write followed her. As a parent and an active volunteer in her church and community, she has a steady flow of ideas to work with. She used her writing skills to teach children in Sunday School—she often wrote plays based on familiar Bible stories for her classes to perform. In her community, she was a volunteer tutor in the Literacy Volunteers of America program. Writing short stories and poems was part of her lesson plans. In her family, she had the responsibility of overseeing the care of six relatives with various forms and stages of dementia for sixteen years, so she became a reluctant expert in Elder Care. Two of her short stories are based on the heartbreak of watching loved ones decline as victims of this terrible disease.

When her husband died in 2009, she moved to Shreveport to adjust to her new life as a widow. She joined a new church and found a place of service in teaching a delightful group of Senior Adult ladies. A friend encouraged her to rekindle her love of writing by joining ACFW-LA. Her association with other writers and incredible support from family and friends inspired her to write devotionals and six published short stories.

Whatever her outlet of expression, God has enabled her to use her writing toolbox in ways she never imagined.

Connect with Beverly Flanders
Smashwords: https://www.smashwords.com/profile/view/
BeverlyFlanders

Other Books by Beverly Flanders
Celebrating the Short Story (2018)
Over the Moon Travel Treasures (2019)
2020 Vision (2020)
Coming of Age (2021)
Second Chances (2022)

ABOUT SUSAN HIERS FOSTER

Susan is the author of two children's books *Because God Tells Me So* about visiting her mother in a nursing home and *Leaping Over Walls* on bullying and forgiveness. In both books, Susan incorporates various family members in her tales, including her grandson John, and grand-dog Vito, a narrating pug.

After two decades spent mostly overseas and in the Washington, DC area with her Army officer husband and children, the Shreveport native returned home. Susan's professional life started in newspapers, including The Shreveport Times, The South Towne Courier, and as city editor of the Leesville Leader. She retired as director of the Noel Neighborhood Food Pantry after 17 years. What started as a job out of her comfort zone eventually became a passion for working with volunteers in serving a community living with food shortages.

Susan enjoys Bible Study Fellowship and volunteers with Embrace Grace, a program for single young women experiencing an unplanned pregnancy. Susan is currently serving as The American Christian Fiction Writers Louisiana chapter's vice president.

As always, Susan's best days are spent with her husband Rick, their adult children and spouses, five active grandchildren, and their on-the-loose pets. Her second-best days are curled up with a book, fully appreciating someone else's hard work.

Connect with Susan Hiers Foster
Facebook: https://www.facebook.com/susan.h.foster.395
Smashwords: https://www.smashwords.com/profile/view/susanhiersfoster

Other Books by Susan Hiers Foster
Because God Tells Me So (2013)
Leaping Over Walls (2021)
2020 Vision (2020)
Coming of Age (2021)
Second Chances (2022)

ABOUT JANN FRANKLIN

Jann Franklin lives in the small town of Grand Cane, Louisiana. Over three hundred other people also live in Grand Cane, and many of Jann's chapters came from her weekly visits at the downtown coffee shop. She would like it on the record that Grand Cane's current mayor and aldermen are nothing like the characters in her book. They are definitely larger than life but in a good way.

She and her husband, John, enjoy Sundays at Grand Cane Baptist Church, dinner with family and friends, and watching the lightning bugs in their backyard. Their kids come to visit when they aren't too busy living their big-city lives.

She graduated from high school in Russellville, another small town in Arkansas. She obtained her accounting degree from Baylor University in Waco, Texas, and moved to Dallas in 1989. She still dabbles in accounting but has taken up writing to satisfy her creative side. Like Jen Guidry, she never appreciated her small-town upbringing until she was encouraged to move back to one. Now she cannot imagine living any other way.

If you ever make it to Grand Cane, stop by 4C Coffee Shop and say "hi." Rhonda Cox and her employees make amazing coffee, and they will save a seat and a smile for you.

Connect with Jann Franklin
Smashwords: https://www.smashwords.com/profile/view/JannFranklin

ABOUT CALVIN HUBBARD

Calvin was born and raised in northwest Louisiana, where he lives today. He is the youngest of five children. His hobby of reading led him to apply for work at a local public library, where he met his wife, Cindy. After dating for four years, they married in 1987. They have one son, who also is married.

Calvin was saved by the Lord Jesus Christ in April 1983. He was called to preach in the summer of 1983 and has been involved in Christian ministry since late 1983. He has served in five churches, in two associations of churches in northwest Louisiana, and on two committees of the Louisiana Baptist Convention. He currently pastors a local Baptist Church and is serving on one associational and one state convention committee. After a nine-year break from college, he returned to school and earned his Bachelor of Arts degree in Christian Ministry from East Texas Baptist University in 1996. He earned his Master of Divinity degree from Southwestern Baptist Theological Seminary in 2007.

He has a passion for sharing God's word in practical ways so that people can be like Jesus and share God's word in their own lives.

He enjoys camping with his wife, reading, learning about new subjects, playing guitar at a basic intermediate level, and trying to paint in acrylics.

Connect with Calvin Hubbard
Blog: www.calvinhubbard.com
Read my story: http://www.whativaluemost.com/Testimony.aspx
Barksdale Baptist Church: https://www.barksdalebaptist.org
Smashwords: https://www.smashwords.com/profile/view/
CalvinHubbard

ABOUT CAROLE LEHR JOHNSON

Carole Lehr Johnson is a veteran travel consultant of more than 30 years and has served as head of genealogy at a local library. She is a member of the American Christian Fiction Writers and a former president of her local ACFW chapter. She has traveled the world and prefers the rolling hills of England. A true Anglophile, Carole loves all things British; thus, her branding, Tea Time for the Heart, revolves around U.K.-based fiction for lovers of tea and scones, castles and cottages, and all things British. Her love of the U.K. has taken her across the pond many times to explore its gorgeous landscapes and buildings as she conducts research for her writing.

Carole lives in Louisiana with her husband and tortoise cat, Lizzy (named after Elizabeth Bennett).

Carole has published a short story in a women's non-fiction anthology, travel articles and photography, several devotionals, won a local writing contest, and has published her third novel, which was a finalist in the 2022 SCWC (South Christian Writer's Conference) Notable Book Awards.

Connect with Carole Lehr Johnson
Website: www.CaroleLehrJohnson.com
Facebook: https://www.facebook.com/
AuthorCaroleLehrJohnson/
LinkedIn: https://www.linkedin.com/in/carole-lehr-johnson-87565555/
Smashwords: https://www.smashwords.com/profile/view/
CaroleJohnson
Email: carole_johnson@att.net

Other Books by Carole Lehr Johnson
Celebrating the Short Story (2018)
Who I Want to Be (2018)
Over the Moon Travel Treasures (2019)
Edge of the Sea (2019)
2020 Vision (2020)
Permelia Cottage (2020)
Coming of Age (2021)
Their Scottish Destiny: A Medieval Scottish Time Travel Novella (2021)
A Place in Time: A Time Travel Novel (2021)
Second Chances (2022)
Burning Sands (2022)

ABOUT MARGUERITE MARTIN GRAY

Marguerite Martin Gray enjoys history, especially when combined with fiction. An avid traveler and reader, she teaches Spanish and French and has degrees in French, Spanish, and Journalism and a MA in English. Marguerite is a member of American Christian Fiction Writers, Abilene Writers Guild, Daughters of the American Revolution, South Carolina Historical Society, and Southern Christian Writers. Always planning her next traveling adventure, she anticipates researching her novels in the setting of her fiction projects. Currently, Marguerite lives in North Louisiana with her husband and three rescue pets. Her two adult children and two grandsons help keep her young and energized.

Connect with Marguerite Martin Gray:
Newsletter: http://eepurl.com/gF-3I1
Website/Blog: http://www.margueritemartingray.com

BookBub: https://www.bookbub.com/authors/marguerite-martin-gray
Facebook: https://www.facebook.com/Marguerite-Martin-Gray-261131773910522/?ref=aymt_homepage_panel
Goodreads: https://www.goodreads.com/author/show/14836211.Marguerite_Martin_Gray
Smashwords: https://www.smashwords.com/dashboard/reassignBook/1071041/assign/MargueriteMartinGray
Email Marguerite at: margueriteg@att.net

Marguerite's published novels include:
Revolutionary Faith Series
Hold Me Close (Book One) (2018)
Surround Me (Book Two) (2019)
Bring Me Near (Book Three) (2019)
Draw Me to Your Side (Book Four) (2020)
Wait for Me (Book Five-the finale) (2021)
The series spans the years 1772-1782 in Charles Town, South Carolina.
Gardens in Time Series
Labor of Love (Book One) (2022) 1560, Florence, Italy
Promise of Purity (Book Two) (2023) 1661, Hampton Court Palace, England

Novella
Keeping Christmas Volume 1 (Anthology of novellas) (2022)

Anthologies
Coming of Age (2021)
Second Chances (2022)

ABOUT TINA MIDDLETON

Since accepting Christ as her Lord and Savior as a young girl, Tina Ann Middleton has been writing poems and essays to share the good news of God's amazing love. Recently she has turned her attention to writing Christian romance with her Forrestville series.

Tina is an avid reader, often reading four or five books at the same time. Her active imagination allows her to picture various scenes, then put them together in a story that not only provides sweet romance but a message of encouragement as well.

She is an active member of American Christian Fiction Writers and enjoys writing short devotionals for the women's ministry at her church.

Tina and her husband, Darran, have been happily married since 1981 and have two grown daughters. They live in northwest

Louisiana and both work at the VA hospital in Shreveport. In her spare time, when she's not reading or writing, she likes to take walks, bake homemade goodies, and work on her jigsaw puzzle app.

Connect with Tina Middleton
Smashwords: https://www.smashwords.com/profile/view/TinaMiddleton

Books by Tina Middleton
The Forrestville Series
Mistaken Target (2020)
Hidden Target (2020)
Unintended Target (2022)
Other Books
Nikki Dog (2018)
Love and Grace: Poems and Essays (2018)

ABOUT C.D. SUTHERLAND

Charles David Sutherland signs his books as C.D. Sutherland. Across three decades, he flew B-52s for the Air Force, where he was known among his fellow warfighters as The Chuck. Then he turned novelist with his *The Chronicles of Susah* series novels, which shook up the fiction world as they defied conventional classification. They blended action and emotional tension with technology and spiritual intrigue in a coming-of-age story wrapped in an epic adventure set in the antediluvian age marking the birth of a new literary genre. His readers called it Antediluvian Steampunk and declared C.D. Sutherland to be its father, establishing him as the Antediluvian Steampunk OG. If you like Biblically-based action adventures for all ages, then look at his books—you'll be glad you did.

Born in the Virginia foothills to a coalminer's son, who long ago joined the Navy to escape a life in the dark Appalachian mines, C.D. Sutherland also joined the military. After high school, he served in the Air Force for thirty-two years, seeing much of the world, flying jets, and doing other things most men have only dreamed about doing.

C.D. Sutherland married the love of his life, and they are well into their 45th year. The two of them are raising a couple of their grandsons. While C.D. Sutherland is a Baptist deacon, author, and ACFW Louisiana chapter President and project manager, he is also the owner and executive editor of Narrow Way Press, LLC, a small independent publishing company. His philosophy for life is to "do the best you can with what you have to work with."

His power verse is:

"I can do all things through Christ which strengtheneth me." (Philippians 4:16 KJV) *

(*note: You can too!)

Connect with C.D. Sutherland
Website: http://cdsutherland.com
Truth Social: https://truthsocial.com/@CDSutherland
LinkedIn: https://www.linkedin.com/in/charles-sutherland-24400a20/
Smashwords: https://www.smashwords.com/profile/view/CDSutherland
Email: realCDSutherland@gmail.com

Other books by C.D. Sutherland:
Biblical Fiction / Steampunk Science Fiction
The Dragoneers: The Chronicles of Susah Book One (2011)

The Lost Dragoneer: The Chronicles of Susah Book Two (2013)
The Last Dragoneer: The Chronicles of Susah Book Three (2014)

Anthologies / Novellas

Celebrating the Short Story (2018)
Over the Moon Travel Treasures (2019)
2020 Vision (2020)
Coming of Age (2021)
Pop, Death, and the Devil (2021)
Second Chances (2022)

Children's

Christmas Candy Cane (2012)

Nonfiction

The Universal Formula for Successful Deterrence (2007)